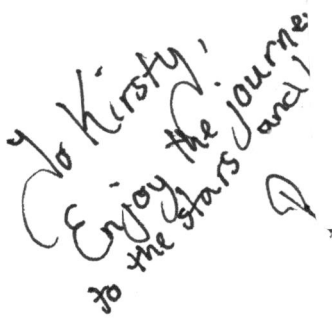

The Star Seed Legacy

Patricia E. Smith

Visit us online at www.authorsonline.co.uk

An Authors OnLine Book

Copyright © Authors OnLine Ltd 2006

Text Copyright © Patricia E. Smith 2006

Cover design by Siobhan Smith ©

All rights reserved. No part of this publication may be reproduced, stored in a retrieval system, or transmitted in any form or by any means, electronic, mechanical, photocopy, recording or otherwise, without prior written permission of the copyright owner. Nor can it be circulated in any form of binding or cover other than that in which it is published and without similar condition including this condition being imposed on a subsequent purchaser.

ISBN 0 7552 0261 9

Authors OnLine Ltd
19 The Cinques
Gamlingay, Sandy
Bedfordshire SG19 3NU
England

This book is also available in e-book format, details of which are available at www.authorsonline.co.uk

Patricia E Smith

Over the last decade or so Patricia has studied and embraced many cultures and the fascinating history, ancient customs and spirituality associated with these cultures.

As a facilitator of workshops, Patricia enjoys bringing people together to experience and share knowledge.

Formerly from St. Andrews, Patricia now lives in Perthshire.

To Paula and Emma,
the two brightest stars in my Galaxy

Chapter 1

Kodo knew there was going to be trouble long before it even started. Menace hung in the air, palpable and pervasive, like some giant bacterial organism waiting to explode and release its poisons on the unsuspecting. Daylight had already given way to that twilight zone before darkness descends to embrace every living thing. There was a sense of acute isolation until a nightjar's weird cry cut through the eerie, lingering stillness. The evening was still mild and balmy, but Kodo felt a chill run through the entire length of his body. There was something else which disturbed him. He was fearful. Not for himself, but for whatever would happen if he couldn't locate the source of that fear. He had never been more conscious of time. He knew he would have to hurry. The grassy verge beside the road was knotted, but he kept to it and his step automatically lengthened. Within minutes he had passed the tall, corroded perimeter fences enclosing the mountainous bings of debris and coal dust. Looming directly behind them, enveloping everything with their brooding, domineering presence, stood the ghostly abandoned silhouettes of a once thriving mining industry. All lay silent now with only the encroaching scrubland and seasonal winds for company. It was a depressing landscape full of scars and ugliness.

There were no lights or cats' eyes to pick out down the centre of the winding country road. Kodo was being careful where he placed his feet. He'd already lost his balance when he stumbled into the protruding, tangled roots of a diseased, long forgotten tree. His mind began to concentrate on other things which had led him here. He was totally unprepared for what was to happen next. Without any warning, the sound of an engine cut right through his thought process, forcing him to focus sharply on his immediate surroundings. It was not a moment too soon. Out of nowhere it seemed, the twin headlights of a pick-up truck suddenly swung directly into view. The glare stunned him, catching him off guard. As the truck veered towards him, he realized it was almost upon him. Only seconds separated the two from impact. Kodo cursed himself.

'Where in the name of hell had that come from?' For the briefest of moments everything looked as though it was being played out in slow motion frames. Kodo wasn't fooled. He was startled, but it was nothing compared to the effect on the driver. He was in a blind panic. Kodo watched as the driver's mobile phone slipped silently through his fingers to land on the passenger's empty seat. Both of his hands reached out to grab the steering wheel. His mouth twisted open and he started screaming obscenities at the top of his voice. Kodo wasn't sure which was worse, his own fear or the anger of the driver. Whether the driver had taken in fully anything about the figure directly in front of him was of no real concern to Kodo right then. He was too busy listening to the voice in his head yelling at him to take some action. 'Move it or you're going to end up beneath the wheels of that truck!' Kodo didn't have to be told twice. He moved sideways away from the direct line of the careering truck and did what he'd done so often throughout his life when he was in physical danger. He shape-shifted. In the time it took the driver to blink, Kodo evaporated into thin air. He turned himself into a common water vole and bolted through the long, toughened grass into a shallow ditch a couple of feet lower down, just as the rim of the front tyre clipped the edge of the grass. Fine gravel and earth spewed up and flew everywhere, showering down on him like minuscule wayward missiles. Kodo's breathing was laboured and his dignity dented but he was alive. He'd been lucky and he knew it. If he was going to see the night through he was going to have to be a lot more vigilant than he had been.

Almost instantaneously his sensory devices picked up on the acrid smell of burning rubber as the wheels of the truck spun trying to gain purchase on the deeply rutted road. High-pitched squeals of brakes making their objections known to such harsh treatment bombarded Kodo from all directions, overriding all other sound. Finally, after it could remonstrate no more, the truck came to a shuddering, screeching halt twenty yards or so away from the sodden clump of knotweed where Kodo was hiding. He sat very still and acclimatized himself to his temporary accommodation. His ears pricked and his whiskers twitched, acutely aware of any vibrational changes around him, conscious of every single whisper of movement. Even at that distance he could hear defiant foul-mouthed abuse coming from the opening in the driver's side window. There was a sharp blast as the driver leant on his horn. He was spitting nails and didn't care who knew it. After the anger came the silence. It didn't last long. Kodo heard the key turn in the ignition, but the engine failed to catch first time. For a moment he was sure the driver was going to reverse and get out of the truck, but he didn't. The engine revved up, emitting a cloud of obnoxious fumes before the truck finally made off at speed.

After reverting back to human form, Kodo very quickly reached the town he'd been heading for and just as swiftly started to work his way through the back streets to the town centre. He was a stranger, yet even at that time of night he went mainly unobserved. All the time he was observing and absorbing every single activity, every little detail. From the family inside their brightly lit living room avidly watching the television, to the couple in a parked car having a heated argument, he missed nothing.

The clothes he wore helped. They were casual and instantly blend-in-able. He liked that, not drawing attention to himself. Just an elderly man with a slight stoop and a walking stick for support. That and a rather decrepit stray mongrel which had somehow latched onto him. It was a mangy looking thing and its ribcage stood out against its emaciated body. Kodo made a half-hearted attempt at chasing it away and distancing himself from it, but in typical canine fashion it remained doggedly determined. In a strange way he found the presence of the dog both familiar and comforting. He vowed that when the night's work was done he would see that the needs of the dog were taken care of. Right now he couldn't deal with any further distractions.

It was stretching the imagination by some great degree to say there was an affluent part of town. When Kodo did come across it he was through it in a matter of minutes. Habitable housing soon gave way to random offices, shops, and then tall tenements. The people became fewer and the area more desolate until eventually only occasional splinters of fragmented light escaped the cracks of the mostly derelict boarded-up buildings. It was no place to linger. He was on the very edge of town now, with just the sound of his boots making contact with the dips and cracks in the pavement and the gentle padding of the dog's footsteps directly behind him. With every step he took his heart grew heavier. He was fast running out of options for finding his source. There was no sign of life at all. No cars, no broken streetlights, nothing. As if to disprove that very thought, in the distance a dog barked. Right after that he heard it: the sound of footsteps running, then a fight breaking out. Harsh voices raised in anger, instantly followed by something he'd hoped not to hear that night. The sound of pain carried on the wind.

'Damn, damn, damn,' Kodo shouted to himself. He sprinted the last few hundred yards along the litter-strewn street and turned into the narrow alleyway. He saw them then, though they were oblivious to his presence. There were five of them in total: four standing, and one on the ground being savagely kicked and beaten by the others. The noise was sickening. Bones must have been splintered and fractured. What was just as horrific was that someone's spirit was being forced into submission. Kodo's heart sank. The punishment which had been carried out had caused great damage. It had been swift and non-negotiable. The outcome had been inevitable. Anonymous thugs with anonymous identities were to blame. Kodo's stomach turned in revolt and revulsion at the scene being played out before his eyes. 'What in God's name had the figure on the ground done that would warrant such a beating? How could people be so brutal? When had the world become so cruel it could turn its back on such savagery?' Then he remembered. He already knew the answer to that. In every land around the globe acts like the one he was witnessing were being carried out on a daily basis. Mob rules ruled, and the weak ended up paying the price.

'Right then you thieving little bastard!' The voice, forceful in its delivery, rang out, bouncing off the walls, echoing as it rose and dipped through the entire length of the alley. As if to emphasize the echo's message further, another vicious boot made contact with flesh. The body on the ground squirmed and tried to break free, but whatever slim window of opportunity had been envisaged proved to be short-lived and completely futile. It was time to try another tack. To minimize the impact from the blows, the body curled up into a foetal position, reducing the body mass considerably. No one seemed to notice. They were working to their own agenda and any attempt at avoidance would swiftly be rectified. The voice picked up where it had left off. All eyes homed in on the figure once again.

'I bet you thought you'd got away from us didn't you? Well ... guess what ... you didn't. Your luck's all run out and now it's pay back time. No more stealing from us. That's a promise. We're going to teach you a lesson you're never going to forget.' It was easy to talk big when the opposition was outnumbered four to one. Just try reversing the tables, Kodo thought. The one doing all the talking was by far the largest and most intimidating. Kodo suspected he was the eldest. At around sixteen he towered over the figure on the ground. It didn't matter much to Kodo who they were or where they had come from. They were a lost cause. His interest was not with them. The others were enjoying the torment of their victim. They continued to egg the 'Big' man on, though in reality none of them needed any encouragement. They were out for blood that night. Defeat was assured and they knew it.

'Yeah, Mikey … that's right. You show the little gimp who's boss. Show him he can't mess with us! That's a shitload of money he stole and we want it back!' One of the cohorts in the beating lunged forward, grabbing hold of the victim's legs, forcing him into a prone position again. With little or no conviction the victim lashed out, still trying to defend himself. Mikey didn't try to conceal his anger and irritation. He bent down and grabbed hold of the writhing child. Kodo realized for the first time that that was all he was: a child of maybe seven or eight years old. He might have been dealt a losing hand, but every ounce of his body yelled out defiance. This only fuelled Mikey's temper even more. In a flash the boy's defiance dissipated.

'Not so clever now, are we gimpy?' Mikey goaded. The child's hand flew to his face as he screamed out in pain. Between the screams he began to sob. The word, though short, dragged out of Mikey's cruelly mocking mouth.

'Aw …' Mikey had his audience. 'Will you look at this guys. Little gwimpy's cwying. What's the matter? No more secret places left to hide away then? No mommy to run home to and wipe away your tears? Well, welcome to the real world poor little orphan boy. There's nowhere for you to go, and no one to even care!' Everyone sniggered as they stopped to see what Mikey would do next. With his face only inches away from the child's, he realized he was getting nowhere fast. Mikey decided to try a different approach. The aggression was temporarily abandoned and the tone of his voice changed to one of gentle persuasion.

'Come on, gimpy. It doesn't have to be like this. We don't want to have to keep on hurting you. Just tell us where the money is and we'll stop this. We'll let you go.' And then as an act of inducement, 'We promise. Don't we guys?'

The group laughed in unison, no one believing for one second there was any real possibility of that happening. One member of the group, who'd so far said very little, must have decided the time was ripe for his contribution to the proceedings. His hooded back was facing the entrance of the alleyway. When he spoke his voice was thin and wheedling. He was quite a bit younger than Mikey, but no less coercive.

'Come on, Mikey. Let it go. Let him go. He's done. You'll get nothing out of him.' He paused, savouring the moment. 'Look, let's just leave him and go to Plan B instead.' There was an audible silence after the words were out. In their minds, the seed had been sown. Everyone turned towards Mikey, desperate to gauge his reaction to the suggestion. Mikey almost seemed relieved. A smirk spread across his face and he pretended to give some real due consideration to the proposal. The pretence disappeared. His response was immediate.

'Well. Well-remembered, bro'. How come I didn't think of that sooner? Okay! Why don't we bring her out. Maybe that'll loosen gimpy's tongue and help refresh his memory a bit. What do you think gimpy? Will we bring your baby sister out and see if she can tell us anything?'

The words were barely out before the boy on the ground tried to roll away, but his legs wouldn't support him. He struggled to sit up, but again his slight frame lacked the reserves. He was in a really bad way and spitting out blood. His voice was so weak it was barely audible. Somehow he found the strength and managed to drag the words from deep within himself.

'I ain't got your money no more, honest. It's gone. All of it. I spent it on food an' a pair of shoes for my sister and me. We was starvin'. We ain't had nothin' to eat for days and she's sick. My sister's really sick. I needed to try an' get her some medicine but it didn't do no good.' It was the last thing the boy managed to say. He slumped forward, face down on the bloody ground. Mercifully his body stilled and he slipped into unconsciousness.

Kodo had seen and heard enough. The hows and whys of the missing money didn't interest him. He went on to automatic pilot. The rage he felt inside went deep, threatening to engulf him. He didn't allow it. The guilt he felt soon overrode all other feelings he had. This was all his fault. He should have found the boy long before these thugs had inflicted their venomous form of instant justice. His voice cut through the air like a pistol shot.

'Step away from the boy!' There was a brief moment of confusion as the perpetrators of the beating realized they were not alone in the alleyway. They immediately closed ranks and stood as a pack, defiant and bristling with aggression. It was dark and dingy but there was just enough light for them to make out the figure of an old man. They began to show some signs of nervousness. That didn't last long. Their arrogance and determination were there for all to see. Even as the boy lay unconscious they were still hellbent on vengeance. Nothing was going to stop them. The fourth figure, who'd so far managed to remain partially hidden from view, stepped out from behind Mikey. Directly behind that figure another figure was being dragged across the filthy ground. It was the boy's little sister and she was so traumatized she couldn't utter a sound. She was tiny and scruffy and very frail. It was difficult to imagine what age she might be.

The person dragging the little girl hauled her to her feet and tightened the grip around her upper body. She had no resistance left in her and didn't put up a struggle. Then Kodo heard a sound far more ominous that any he'd heard that night. It terrified him. There was a dull click as the blade of the flick-knife sprung open. He watched in horror as it was placed right up against the little girl's neck.

'Sod off, granddad! This isn't your business!' When Kodo heard the voice he was shocked. Dressed in dark clothing like the others and wearing a baseball cap with the peak to the back, the figure took a couple of steps forward. It was a young girl not much older than the boy on the ground.

In that instant Kodo the old man became Kodo as he really was. The stoop disappeared and the years and initial disguise slipped away as he pulled himself up to his full height and size. The alley filled with brilliant white light and the pack saw for the first time the true form and identity of their adversary. Kodo stood, feet apart. He was tall, very tall, and though he wasn't bulky, none could mistake the sheer physical presence of the man. His muddy blond hair was tied back from his olive coloured skin and his green eyes, which had pierced the souls of many with just one glance, were unrelenting as they stared fixedly ahead. Above his left cheekbone, a short scar, faded by time, was the only discernable mark on his part-oriental complexion. The garments he wore were pale creamy grey and loose fitting. Around his waist a broad black linen belt held them together. On his feet were softened leather shoes which looked like slippers but weren't. He was a little like a modern day samurai warrior. The only difference was he carried no armour for protection, nor any sword for fighting. In his right hand he held a long wooden staff. That was all he would need.

He heard the snuffling of the stray mongrel as it worked its way down the alleyway and came to stand by his side. A memory was triggered inside his brain but it was fleeting and he couldn't quite grasp it. Kodo was comfortable with the silence which followed, though what the reaction of the group would be to his command he was unable to predict at this precise point. If they were sensible they would turn round and hightail it right out of there, but as he very soon realized, they weren't sensible. Foolhardy, Mikey managed to get some sort of handle over his fear, and what was just as alarming was the fact that the girl with the knife decided to attempt to back him up. Kodo tried again. Not taking his eyes off the group for one second, he reiterated his previous request. There could be no mistaking the authority or underlying intent in his voice.

'Let the girl go now and you'll come to no harm!' Kodo stood perfectly still waiting for the inevitable deliverance of the fighting four's acceptance. As if to strengthen his stance, though there was no need, the stray mongrel chose that precise moment to do a little shape-shifting of his own. The starving docile-looking animal merged with the energy of another and turned into 'Wolf.' Not just any old wolf either, but Gaelun's Wolf. Now that was something Kodo hadn't been expecting. He smiled for the first time that night. Trust Gaelun to send back-up, even though it hadn't been requested. He was grateful nonetheless. Wolf was impressive. The tips of his ears reached the middle of Kodo's thighs and his long bushy tail when it was extended was almost the length of Kodo's arm. His thick lustrous white coat was tinged with gold and, when on the rare occasion it was asked of him, he was strong enough to bring down a grown man. Right now though, the group could only guess at what he was capable of. Like Kodo he stood resolutely still. The soft scarred pads of his large splayed paws loosely gripped the ground beneath him. All the weight of his body was finely balanced ready to spring into action. Though Wolf might appear completely relaxed he was capable of moving with a speed and directness which left people stunned, or, should they be on the receiving end, terrified. He managed to look all the more intimidating when his hackles rose and his lips curled back to reveal some mighty incisors and a long dark tongue.

Though it had never been in doubt, it was important for the group to realize their brand of justice was now over. The younger boys backed off, leaving Mikey and the girl to fend for themselves. Nothing more was said as Kodo realized the remaining two weren't prepared to back down completely. Even against such odds they were crazy, crazy enough to prove a point.

The move was almost imperceptible, but Kodo and Wolf were onto it at once. The girl went to stick the knife into the little girl's throat at the very same time Mikey made a grab for the boy on the ground. Kodo was swifter than both of them. He raised his staff and pointed it straight at them. Two blinding flashes of light moved with such speed and force that Mikey and the girl didn't even have time to think. Their bodies were lifted high in the air, then slammed back down against the side of one of the buildings. The knife lay discarded a few feet away from the girl's inert body. Both she and Mikey were out cold on the same bloodied ground their helpless victim lay on. The brutality and ugliness of their night's vicious administerings were at an end. It was over.

Wolf caught the little girl as she slipped from the clutches of her captor. She was terrified, on the point of passing out. Wolf's mighty jaws immediately slackened as he released the girl and lowered her gently onto the ground. He stood over her watching her, wanting to absorb her pain. Her mouth opened and she screamed her own silent scream. Her eyes were wide and vacant as she relived in her own childlike mind the events in the alleyway. Kodo, who was kneeling down beside her brother, reached over towards her. She didn't even flinch. He placed a finger on her tiny heart and let his energy flow straight into her. The last things she saw before she closed her eyes were Kodo's smile and Wolf as he leaned forward to lick the small wound on her neck.

There was no time for small talk. That could come later. Kodo rolled the boy over and gently lifted him up, cradling him just as a baby would be cradled. He was as light as a feather and smelled awful. Underneath all the dirt and blood Kodo saw the bruises and felt the damaged bones. His shoulder was dislocated, several ribs fractured and he was bleeding internally. When he looked at the boy's legs he knew instantly why he'd been so cruelly taunted. One of his legs was malformed, and, for whatever reason, because no treatment had taken place it had remained that way. This poor boy hadn't stood a chance. All that was going to change. Kodo was ready. He looked at the little girl and then at Wolf.

'If I strap her to your back can you carry her to the portal? I don't want to harm the boy further by carrying her as well. Will you manage?'

'I'll manage,' replied Wolf.

Kodo worked silently and with great speed. Time really was of the essence. Both he and Wolf knew that. He had one final thing to do before they left the memories of the alleyway behind and set off. His hand covered the boy's head, and just as he had done for the little girl he did for her brother. Energy spread through the boy and as the colour returned to his face, Kodo knew the boy would survive. There was a moment when the boy seemed to realize someone was helping him and not beating him. His eyes opened and he looked into the stranger's face. The boy forced the laboured whispered words out of his small parched mouth.

'Where am I, mister? Who are you?' It was too much. His lids came down and his eyes closed again. Kodo bent his head down and whispered softly back to him.

'It's all over. You're safe now and your sister's safe. Wolf and I are here. We've come to take you both home to your family.'

Chapter 2

The night was calm, the sky ablaze with limitless possibilities and expectations. Swathe upon swathe of luminous stars and stardust stretched out into the realms of forever and beyond. Some stars were so small they were undetectable to the naked eye. Others which went to create the mightier, more recognizable constellations stood out in relief against a backdrop of inky intensity. A vibrant, pulsating, velvety mass suspended like crystal firefly globes and so low in places they dipped down and let the brilliance of their rays spread out and merge into the faded horizon. This was a living, ever-evolving canvas brushed by phenomenal depth of beauty.

Arrianna felt all she had to do was reach out and the stars would be within her grasp. All her life she had felt the pull of the stars. It was a powerful connection and one she likened in many ways to the relationship the stars shared with the magnetic forces of the galaxies. She was also drawn to that power without fully understanding why. Just thinking about it made the tiny fine hairs on the back of her neck stand up. Relaxed muscles in her shoulders suddenly stiffened and contracted as sharp jagged edges of a shiver shot through her. In one fluid movement she pulled her knees tight up against her upper body, trying without much success to block out the sensation. She knew she should move away from the narrow window seat into the comforting warmth of her bed, but she couldn't. She was too terrified to close her eyes, too terrified of the images she knew would surface. Her mind was in such turmoil it threatened to overwhelm her. She could find solace in nothing. Adrenalin had kept her going for the past seventy-two hours, but emotionally she was now running on near empty. When she had reached that place deep within herself, a place where few would ever wish to venture, any options she felt she had left open to her fragmented and then dissolved. It was easy to give in and succumb when the insidious icy tendrils of darkness came and took hold. Never had she felt so alone. For the third time in her young life she was staring very real personal loss straight in the face. She couldn't go through this again.

When she was just fourteen both her parents had drowned in a freak boating accident. Arrianna had been there when it happened. A day's sailing off Hunters' Break had turned into tragedy in a matter of minutes. They had seen the storm approach and as the wind started to pick up they turned about and headed back towards the small inlet where her father moored the boat. At this point no one was unduly worried. They were all experienced sailors and knew this particular coastline like the back of their hands. They knew they could outrun the storm, but the forces of nature were against them that day. Arrianna was never sure just how it happened. Every time she tried to play back the events of the day in her mind, the shutters came down; everything was blocked out. She remembered only the weight of the boom as it swung around, catching her across the side of her head. There was a dull, heavy cracking sound, then everything went black. The next thing she knew she was battling the waves with only her bright yellow lifejacket keeping her afloat, away from the vicious undercurrents which would pull her down and under to the ocean floor. Blood was pouring down into her eyes and her head felt like the inside of a pressure cooker about to explode. She screamed out for her parents, trying to pinpoint their exact location, but it was a futile exercise. The waves had become so powerful they kept picking her up out of the water and hurling her straight back down into their heaving vortex. When she heard her mother's faint voice rise above the waves some distance off, she found a renewed energy. Her head swivelled round and instinctively sought the location of the voice. The last image, though she didn't know it at the time, was of her beautiful raven-haired mother Eleina shouting out across the void between them, to swim for her life. She felt relief knowing her parents were all right. They were strong swimmers, they'd be okay. Arrianna turned and started to swim towards the shoreline. Halfway there she passed out again. When she did finally come to, she was back on shore with Grandfather down on both knees leaning over her. He must have been the one who'd placed her on her side in the recovery position. His breathing was heavy and laboured and his clothes were saturated and covered with sand and slippery strands of fine seaweed thrown up by the waves. Every part of Arrianna ached as she struggled to sit up on the shifting sand. Off to the left of Grandfather, half in and half out of the water, Arrianna could make out what looked to be the shredded deflated remains of two life jackets. Her mouth opened partially as the breath caught in the back of her throat. As realization swiftly dawned and the implications of that realization registered, she opened her mouth wider and the scream came.

'No–o–o! No–o!' Grandfather reached out to restrain her. He pulled her towards him and held her so tight she thought her ribs would crack. No further confirmation was needed as to the awful outcome of the day. When Arrianna looked at Grandfather his face told her all she needed to know. Nausea swept through her like a runaway steam train and just as swiftly her body went limp. She felt numb and in total shock. Frantic though her thoughts were, she managed some small degree of control as her eyes sought out and found those of her young brother. He was just standing staring straight at her. She thought her heart would shatter into a thousand pieces when she looked into his eyes. There were no tears but the haunted, confused look on his small pale face would stay with her forever.

Grandfather took up the reins of being their guardian and over the next several years he loved them and looked after them. He gave up his travelling to far-flung places and concentrated on being the best guardian he could be. They all learnt to adjust to the changes in their lives. They united and grew together and learnt to laugh again.

Arrianna had just celebrated her twentieth birthday when tragedy struck for the second time. Grandfather went to bed one night and simply never woke up again. Theo was only thirteen years old. Both had been devastated beyond words when they realized they were to be deprived of the one guiding light left in their lives. It was a bitter, bitter blow and one they were still coming to terms with three months later. Family friends had instantly rallied around offering loving support and advice, trying to cushion the pain and the brutal effects of so sudden a loss. In the immediate aftermath it had helped, but eventually everyone needed to return to their own lives and some sense of normalcy. For Arrianna and Theo, living was the reality. It could not be put on hold until they were ready.

There was never any question in Arrianna's mind that she and Theo would continue to live in the only home they'd known, and that she would take over the parenting of Theo. It's what her parents would have wanted and Grandfather would have wanted what was best for them both. She could combine her study of archaeology and still look after Theo. She knew it wasn't an easy road she'd chosen, and though she hid it well, the pressure she felt to emulate her parents and Grandfather was enormous.

At first she and Theo came together, numbed and freshly desensitized by their pain; a couple of lost souls in a sea of foggy grief. They shared their rawness and vulnerability and to a degree warded off their demons of uncertainty. Then a few weeks ago, all that changed. Theo started withdrawing into himself. He became difficult and non-communicative. What few responses Arrianna did manage to elicit from him were either monosyllabic or tinged with such anger it hurt. Each day became an endurance test. Arrianna wanted to help change the consistent, highly charged atmosphere which existed between them, but she couldn't. Whatever she said or did was always the wrong thing. Theo refused point-blank to discuss it. The strain began exacting a high toll and Arrianna began to seriously doubt her own ability to turn things around. Every day they argued about silly, inconsequential things. It was wearing both of them down. Theo was unwilling or unable to accept that his behaviour was in equal measure both obnoxious and distressingly unwarranted. Arrianna hoped he'd grow out of it and return to being the mild-mannered, stroppy teenager she knew and loved. It never happened. Theo stormed out of the house early one afternoon after yet another really unpleasant scene. He didn't return that day or the next. He had disappeared without a trace. When, by day three, the police had failed to throw up any information at all on his whereabouts, he was declared as officially missing. To Arrianna it was a step too far, a clear sign in her eyes that destiny's intervention had breached her last defence. How much more was she expected to deal with? How much more could she take? Guilt kicked in as Arrianna blamed herself. 'What ifs' saturated her mind. She was living in a horrible nightmare and she wanted it to stop. She desperately wanted Theo to walk through the front door and put everything right again.

By ten o'clock that night the house finally became mercifully quiet. The police, the neighbours and the friends who'd been drifting in and out of the house for days had finally gone home for the night. Arrianna marvelled at just how amazing everyone had been. The support had been unswerving and unconditional. So many had come forward to join in the search for Theo. All had remained positive, though she was finding it difficult to share their optimism.

Now she was just relieved to be on her own and let the silence embrace her. It didn't last long. Three sharp blasts of the bell followed in rapid succession by two more, sounded the arrival of someone at the front door. She debated whether to ignore it but when it rang again she knew she couldn't. It could very well be the police … it might even be Theo. Her heart sank a little as she walked through the house switching on lights as she went. The outside porch lights were the last. She opened the heavy door, prepared for anything but in her heart expecting the worst.

What she wasn't prepared for was the figure in the doorway. She blinked then blinked again at the sight of the man standing before her. It was Kodo. Arrianna opened her mouth to say something, but the words wouldn't come. No words were needed between them. Not then. Kodo stepped into the house and with his arms about her he just held her close to him. His energy shot through the maze of pain and confusion she felt and his strength absorbed the great racking sobs. With an arm still around her, he led Arrianna over to one of the comfy old armchairs by the large open stone fireplace. Kneeling down in front of her, Kodo lovingly wiped away the tears, and as though to reassure her he gently brushed her cheek with the back of his large smooth hand. It was a tender moment full of poignancy and understanding. He lifted her chin and looked at her, taking in everything about her. The puffiness around her eyes and the pinched look in her face told of the stress she had been under, and he knew because he'd held her she probably hadn't been eating properly or taking care of herself. Kodo felt a pain tug at the edges of his heart. His poor, beautiful Arrianna. He wanted to look after her and protect her forever, but for the time being he just continued to look at her. She was normally so vibrant and full of life but now she appeared almost fragile. Hanging down loosely about her shoulders was her long, dark hair. It was wispy and unruly, just as her mother's had been and she had her father's large, blue-grey unfathomable eyes. She was tall and her slimness accentuated that and made her appear even taller. She'd changed a great deal since he'd last seen her earlier that year. That she was sad was not in doubt, but there was an elusive air of something yet to come about her. Her beauty was subtle and wild, but Kodo knew it was the beauty within her which was the truly special thing. She had so much of her parents and her grandfather in her, it was unnerving.

Arrianna did some observations of her own as she familiarized herself again with the features of Grandfather's closest friend and ally. He was a lot younger than Grandfather, but the two had a great bond which united them. Age was no barrier. Here was someone she'd known all her life. To Theo and herself he was family, someone to be trusted and loved. If ever she needed Kodo around, it was now. She felt the tension in her body subside and start to drain away. A thought flashed through her mind, a thought as so often in the past she'd asked herself and could find no real answer to. What was it about this man who could still her heart and fill her with the peace she longed for? In response to her own questioning the corners of her mouth turned up, then tentatively, almost shyly, she smiled at Kodo. When she spoke to him, her voice was soft and filled with so many different emotions. She looked straight at him.

'Oh, Kodo ... thank God you're here. I hoped and prayed you'd come, that somehow you'd know we needed you here, needed your help. Where have you been? Why couldn't we get hold of you?' Arrianna hesitated, as if remembering some unsaid thing, some memory they shared. She turned her head away, unable to meet Kodo's enquiring gaze. The telltale quiver in the lips returned as her crushed, bruised eyes threatened to fill up and spill over with tears once again. She lifted her head. Her voice this time was no more than a whisper.

'Why didn't you come when Grandfather died? ... He was your friend and you didn't turn up. What happened to keep you away from something like that? How could you not come?'

Kodo heard every single syllable, every single word. The muscles on the side of his face tightened as he listened to the pain in Arrianna's voice. He apportioned no blame to the rebuke. It was probably justified. There was a flicker of some strong emotion in Kodo's eyes, but whatever it was remained inaccessible and closed off. Arrianna saw it though, and felt remorse. She hadn't meant to sound accusatory.

'I'm sorry, Kodo ... I didn't mean to ...'

'No, you're right. I should have come. I should have been here for you and Theo.'

She watched him lean back, putting all his weight on his heels, then rise effortlessly to his feet. He didn't bother to untie his shoes. He just kicked them off where he stood. The jacket was next and that he slung in one single motion over the back of the sofa. This amused Arrianna. It was such a male thing to do. Why did boys and grown up men alike feel obliged to create mess. Was there an in-built trait in their psyche which made them like that?

The lighting in the room was soft and subdued, a bit like the mood and Arrianna noticed for the first time since his arrival just how drawn and haggard Kodo was. He looked as shattered as she felt. That was a strange phenomenon for Kodo. To Arrianna he'd always appeared ageless. She remembered once as a child guilelessly asking him, 'How old are you really, Kodo? Grandfather says you're ancient.' Much to her frustration, he refused to give her a direct answer. He'd smiled, amused at her directness and his eyes had crinkled up. He'd ruffled her hair and simply replied, 'Not old, little Arrianna. Not old.' Tonight though, he looked old. Without asking her if she wanted one, Kodo proceeded to pour them both a drink. He handed her one with a wry, bemused look on his face.

'Go on, you look as though you need something. I know I do. Besides, it'll help you to relax ... just don't drink it in a oner, okay?' He raised his own glass to his mouth and drank deeply, then set it down on the small ornate table by Arrianna's side. The other large wing-back chair which was always regarded as Grandfather's chair, was dragged across the worn, timbered flooring. Kodo placed it so that he was directly facing Arrianna. After the fringed velvet cushion was satisfactorily plumped up, Kodo sat down and made himself at home. It was almost like old times, but both knew in their heart of hearts that it would never be like that again.

Grandfather's malt did the trick and Kodo's whole body relaxed as the warm amber liquid hit the spot. He leaned over towards Arrianna and placed his strong, long hand on top of hers.

'Arrianna ... I know this is difficult for you having to repeat the same things over and over again, but I need to hear this. So ... tell me about Theo and everything that led up to his disappearance. Don't miss out anything. I have to know exactly what went on here after your grandfather's death, every little detail, no matter how insignificant. It's really important you remember who Theo saw, where he went. Did you notice anything unusual, any strangers about? Think hard, Arrianna. A lot more than you realize may be at stake here.'

And so Arrianna started to relive all the terrible events leading up to that night. Kodo listened, but said little. When she faltered or was unsure, he pressed her to be more specific. He wanted nothing left out. By the time Arrianna had finished, she was distraught again and completely exhausted. Every vestige of colour had left her face as she sat back and rested her head against the fabric of the chair. The thought of Theo being out there somewhere on his own was killing her. How could he have just disappeared off the face of the earth like that? Why had the police found no new leads? Where was he?

Kodo was restless and preoccupied as he paced up and down, sifting through every piece of information Arrianna had given him. He was quiet for so long Arrianna wondered what he would come up with that she hadn't already thought a million times herself. Unbeknownst to Arrianna, Kodo had come to a decision he'd been struggling with for hours. He was going to have to tell her. Just how or how much he'd just have to trust to Arrianna and his instincts about her. He knew her almost as well as she knew herself, but would she believe him, would that be enough? There were no alternatives left open to Kodo and he knew that. The timing was all wrong, but he no longer had that luxury. If they were to save Theo she would have to be told. This was not going to be easy.

He calmed his thoughts but when he spoke there was an urgency in his voice which Arrianna had never heard before. She was sleepy but still sensed something had changed.

'Arrianna, I need you to be strong for just a little bit longer. Please just sit and let me speak. You need to know this and I'll try and keep everything as simple as possible. I have things to say to you, things unlike anything you'll have heard before. All your life you've been safe and protected from such knowledge but recent events and Theo's disappearance have changed all that. The Council decided you shouldn't be kept in the dark any longer. We must all pull together on this. A lot of things are going to happen to you which you'll find extraordinary and impossible to understand. I need you to trust me Arrianna as you've never trusted me before. I need to know that no matter what I tell you, you must believe me absolutely. There can be no doubts in your mind. This is the most important decision you'll ever make. Your life and Theo's will depend on your answer. Do you trust me to that degree, Arrianna? Will you place your life in my care and come with me?' He waited and listened to the silence which followed.

Arrianna was, as Kodo expected, confused by his words, but she knew as soon as Theo's name was mentioned that she'd do anything and go anywhere to get him back. Deep down in her heart she knew Kodo would protect her and see that she came to no harm. There was something other than that though. She knew with a conviction borne out of family and a lifetime's friendship of her grandfather that she could trust this man with her life.

A simple 'Yes' was all it took. Kodo stood still as the enormity of the reply sunk in. So, he'd been right about Arrianna. She did trust him. He was relieved and his smile acknowledged that.

Time was precious and none was wasted.

'Right then, Arrianna. I have some things to see to and you need to sleep. We need to be away from here long before the sun comes up. Now, lie down on the sofa, close your eyes and sleep. You're done in. I need you strong, ready to face the day. Okay?'

Arrianna was too weary not to comply when Kodo covered her with a small woollen rug off the sofa. Then Kodo did what Arrianna thought was a strange thing. He placed the palm of his hand over her heart and held her gaze with one of his own. His voice was soft and gentle.

'Sleep well Arrianna,' he said as he leant back into his armchair and picked up his half empty glass from the side table. In a matter of seconds Arrianna's eyes grew heavy and a wonderful glowing warmth spread through her. Just before sleep overtook her, she remembered to ask Kodo something which was puzzling her. 'You haven't said yet, but where exactly are we going? Where are you taking me to and who are the Council?' She turned her head sideways to look at him but his face was partially hidden by lamplight. He had the strangest look on his face. Arrianna could swear he was grinning when he looked straight at her and said very matter of factly, 'I'm taking you to see your grandfather ... where else?'

Chapter 3

Arrianna wasn't sure if she was conscious or not. She thought she might be. Her mind was saying yes but her eyes were deceiving her and telling another very different story. She had felt herself rapidly slipping in and out of a landscape which was so fantastical she knew it had to be that. Just a dream. How else would she have known that everything around her was so alien a concept she found the very idea of reconciling herself and coming to terms with it a near impossibility. It was beyond all realms of her limited understanding and difficult to gain any real perspective on. This was unlike anything she had known or had knowledge of.

Time seemed to be standing still and Arrianna had no conception of reality anymore. She was so far removed from herself she knew she had to be in another dimension. Her body began the gradual process of filling with light as it started to respond and radiate at a higher vibration. Something told her a delicate state of transference and balance existed when she found herself suffused and bathed with a new deep inner glow, which had little to do with feeling good about herself and more about raising the galactic vibration.

In complete awe and disbelief Arrianna wondered at her improbable isolation, cocooned in the clear, rainbow crystal triangle cutting a pathway through the heaving mass and swirls of stardust and clouds of gases. Being trapped within this triangular, modular space was having the weirdest effect on her. There should have been noise as she sped through the debris of the galaxies, but all she could hear was the echo of her own heartbeat. Every cell in her body was at that very point in time being restructured and realigned to adapt with her rapidly evolving environment. She was in her own uncharted no man's land with little idea of anything. A spasm of something akin to trepidation swept over her as a cold creeping paralysis skirted and tried to infiltrate the edges of her mind. All credibility was abandoned as Arrianna surrendered herself into allowing what was going to happen, happen. There could be no stopping off now on this galactic roller coaster of a journey. Even supposing it were at all possible, returning to the security of her own safe, sane world just was not an option.

Her heart rate began to slow down to a gentle, more rhythmic pace, calming all her thoughts and confusion. Everything was happening so quickly, but even in that there was a contradiction. Scenes were being played out in apparent slow motion. It was bizarre. In an instant the triangle slowed down until it was almost stationary. Though nothing was visible, Arrianna felt that whatever was responsible for propelling and steering her had been put into neutral. Now she was simply hovering, dipping, then hovering some more.

As she looked down from this wondrous, magical free fall, a vast stellar crystalline landscape of deep cavernous ravines and gorges and large expansive spaces began to emerge and open up before her. She felt a subtle shift in her body's energy. A spark of some past emotion or experience. A feeling of familiarity and recognition which she somehow took great comfort from. She tried absorbing everything in her view but quickly realized there was only so much she could take in.

Scattered along the landscape like iridescent living jewels fallen from the skies, small brilliant clusters of oddly shaped structures rose up out of the ground to meet her. They were a long way beneath her but she knew they had to be dwellings of some kind. Was this the first inkling of habitation? Something stirred inside Arrianna when she looked at the structures. Heading off away from them were narrow ribbon-like strips of what could have been roads. It was difficult to tell. Far in the distance Arrianna saw incredible mountain peaks which, defying all gravity, stretched out before her as far as her eyes would allow her to see. They were breathtaking and utterly hypnotic. Momentarily she was dazzled and almost blinded as their surfaces moved and shifted, sending their reflection bounding straight back on to her. Light washed over her then in waves. This was a strange ethereal, surreal place trapped between worlds where nothing was as it seemed. The atmosphere was unquestionably different and the air, if that was how it could be described within such restricted parameters, left Arrianna with a peculiar mixture of light-headedness and nausea. She remembered rationalizing that to herself. If she could actually feel so wretched, she must still be alive! It was as sobering a thought as it was exhilarating.

Arrianna's next recollection was of being confined in a room or chamber which had no windows, walls or doors. Energy alone created the sense of shape and form. Perhaps she'd been placed here in order to make her feel a little more secure with her surroundings. She just didn't know. The ceiling had gone and she found herself staring, not at a myriad of stars, but out into a clear, vacuous space of nothingness where everything was still and silent. A gentle, floating motion rocked her body as it came to rest on a bed of the softest covering imaginable. It was like lying on a bed of clouds where once again energy was responsible for the illusion of outlines. The covering was the sole concession to colour in a room with a palette depicting every aspect of white imaginable to man. There was no sense of light and shade, just whites blending and merging into other whites. Arrianna was curious to know what the covering was made of, what it felt like to the touch. Her hand disappeared into its folds as she tried to grasp it. When she pulled her hand out she was rewarded. Immediately she was struck by its weightless liquid properties. It was fascinating to watch as it slipped through her fingers like finely spun threads on a shimmering golden waterfall. For the briefest of seconds droplets hung suspended before flowing slowly downwards to settle once more on the surface.

Arrianna was dressed in a long, softly draped gossamer lined robe and her feet were bare. She felt completely at peace with herself. The endless restrictions and boundaries she'd placed in her mind were suddenly freed. It was a liberating feeling, accepting what destiny had in store for her. She stretched and wiggled her toes, luxuriating in the sensation as they too disappeared into the covering. Laughter rose up in the back of her throat and she began to giggle.

Wherever Arrianna was, the place held no fear for her. She accepted that she was being given only the minutest of glimpses of this strange and wonderful environment. So far this one room wasn't enough to base any conclusion on. What lay beyond her invisible walls, she wondered? There had to be something greater than the confined imagery of this space. She instinctively knew that there was. Her heart began speaking to her as a feeling she'd known so often in her dreams swept over her and embraced her. The lifetime longings of discovering who she was and where she'd come from were in that second confirmed in her mind. Intuition and something much deeper told her she was finally at home in the land of her own people.

'Arrianna, it's time to open your eyes. Wake up now, you're okay. Everything is going to be all right.' Through all the flashbacks and distorted images bouncing about in her mind, Arrianna felt the words sink in deep, penetrating her sleep-induced brain. The timbre and inflection in the voice told her one thing. It was Kodo. She knew then she really was back with the person she trusted and felt safest with. Her eyelids felt heavy and sluggish, as though she'd been asleep for a very long time, but her body was buzzing with an energy, an aliveness she'd never felt before. If ever proof were needed that she had integrated fully with her newest environment, that time was now. All the madness she thought had been a figment of her imagination was a reality. She was alive and living it right now.

Arrianna sat up and swung her legs down as she turned to face Kodo. She knew she shouldn't have been surprised considering everything she'd seen and been through, but she was. Kodo was there all right, but it was a very different Kodo and she was totally unprepared to see what she did. She could have sworn she felt the walls of the room expand to accommodate his presence. Like her, he was dressed in loose flowing white garments, but that was where all similarities ended. Arrianna's eyes widened and her mouth parted. She was stunned. This person standing beside her was magnificent. A 'Being' of light so incredible it took the breath straight out of her lungs. Physically it was easy to identify him as Kodo. It was all the 'other things' which told Arrianna she was in the presence of something she'd only every heard of in works of fiction. She felt foolish for being so unutterably naïve about the real Kodo she'd known, and she was humbled in a way at his 'mightiness' or whatever one could call it. Speech failed her.

Kodo was surrounded by a gently pulsating aura of white golden flickering rays. His entire body was light and it flowed from him straight into Arrianna's heart. She bent her head, overcome, trying to conceal the confusion, the sensation, unable to meet his gaze a second longer. Kodo understood and was gentle and compassionate. He cupped her face in his hands until she faced him once more, then smiled that irrepressible smile of his. He reached down to hug her and Arrianna felt herself almost melt and become absorbed by the energy which was Kodo. The effect was instant as her body filled with an even more radiant light and strength. It was such a natural gesture on Kodo's behalf, but for Arrianna it was a powerful, indefinable, sharing moment which would change her life forever. He let her go, then stood back a little.

'Not quite what you were expecting, I take it?' Then he laughed. It was so infectious Arrianna couldn't ignore it. She could look at him again. He came and sat companionably beside her and immediately she knew everything he'd said to her really would be all right. There were so many questions, each rushing to surface above the other. She didn't know where to begin. Thoughts of Theo came flooding back to gnaw away at her conscience. Was he the reason she was here now? Recollections returned of the conversation she'd had with Kodo in the living room of her home. Had he mentioned Grandfather or had she just imagined that? Where was she? What was this place? Who was this Kodo and why had he brought her here? The questions were interminable and just kept coming.

Kodo watched as a host of emotions played across Arrianna's face. She was completely unnerved and who could blame her? It was time to help her out. Kodo respected her feelings and was careful to be as succinct as possible with his words.

'It's probably easiest Arrianna if you just listen while we sit. I'll try to answer some of the things rushing around in that head of yours. There's so much you need to know, but honestly I promise, in your time here all your questions will be answered. You'll come to understand and accept all your experiences no matter how they might appear to you. In a very short space of time you'll become so at ease and so much a part of everything around you, you'll barely notice. It will become what it is, second nature. You're already a good part of the way there. Once before you placed your trust in me, so just trust me on this, okay?'

Kodo paused for a second or two. It was important that her mind was open to what he was about to say.

'I need to speak to you about this place.' Kodo opened his hands and gestured towards the room. 'You need to know where it is and why we both come to be here. First of all you need to know your own history ... it's important. So tell me, do you think you're ready to hear the story of your ancestors? Do you want to know where you come from, where we all came from and how we come to be here right now?'

Arrianna's heart lurched when she heard those words. A strange excitement built up in the pit of her stomach. She lost herself in the deep, spiralling vortex of Kodo's eyes and nodded. What was it about him that could affect her so?

'Of course I want to know' she whispered, almost silently. 'You know I do.' Kodo picked up where he had left off.

'Well ... welcome to Astaurias. Just as you thought, this is only one tiny part of something very much greater. When we've finished talking I'll show you just how magnificent this place truly is and how special a place it is going to be in your heart from now on. This is my home and home to the 'Star Beings'. I am one of many such beings who transcend all space, dimension and time. We come from the stars and inhabit this one particular star. There are seven stars within the group which forms Astaurias and each star has its own 'Star Beings'. Each star is looked over by only the mightiest of Star Beings. On this star it is Gaelun. The others I will teach you about later. For the time being, it's best that I keep things simple.' Arrianna sat totally transfixed at the revelations. All those years of yearning and the deep inner knowing about her connection with the stars were all at once realized. Kodo continued.

'Way back aeons ago, before people inhabited Earth, the Star Beings evolved and formed small nuclei in the numerous star systems throughout the galaxies. When man did begin to inhabit Earth, and other beings other universes, the Star Beings decided to come together and settle under one roof, so to speak. That roof was … is Astaurias. At that time we neither wanted nor needed to be in any other place. Our home was in the stars with the stars. From the beginning the Star Beings were granted incredible powers which we still have to this day. With time some chose those powers to incarnate on Earth. They chose to experience mortality. When their lives there were completed they were able to return to Astaurias. They became immortal again. In Earth years they lived a lifetime, but in star time it was a mere blinking of the eye. The descendants of the Star Beings on Earth each lived out their lives on Earth and remained there when their lives were over. Only in exceptional times are people of Earth brought to the stars and if they wish they are given the option of returning to Earth once more. We are living in just such times and that is why you've been brought here. It was never our intention to involve you in any of this, but you are already involved even if you don't realize it just yet. When Earth itself, or the people of Earth are placed in mortal danger we have the power to intervene. Only the seven mightiest Beings who come together to form the Council have the authority to make that decision. They don't do this lightly. Many beings have abused their powers and been corrupted while on Earth. Some have literally gone underground. Others have created portals into parallel universes and still live there today, plotting and scheming and seizing power for themselves. Largely we tolerate them because they have no real power, but the one who calls himself Karalan has amassed so much power, the havoc and chaos he is unleashing on Earth cannot be allowed to continue. He'll do anything in his power to corrupt the souls of innocents. He's stealing not just Earth's future but your future as well. He's bent on absolute power and the destruction of all that is good. He will not be allowed to succeed.' Kodo stopped speaking. He'd prepared her as best he could. Was she going to be strong enough?

'There's no easy way of telling you this, Arrianna. Karalan is the one who has Theo. We've only just found out that his 'Watchers' took Theo on the day he walked out of your family home. None of us could have foreseen this happening. We weren't prepared for it.' Instantly the atmosphere changed perceptibly as the implication of Kodo's words sank in. Arrianna's relief at being told Theo was alive was tempered with how long Kodo had known this. The realization of the ease with which he'd lied to her shocked Arrianna. She was seething at his apparent deception and duplicity. He had deliberately kept the truth from her about Theo and Karalan and she was furious at herself for being so gullible. Why hadn't he told her when he came to see her? What value did he place on the words he'd spoken? What was the point about trust? Where was his trust then? It was alright for her to trust him, but not apparently the other way round. There was an audible 'Wha–a–at?' in the room. Arrianna felt as if Kodo had struck her with his own hand. The pain she felt went deeper than normal hurt. She rose to her feet and faced him. She felt shocked and let down and she didn't wholly believe him. Anger oozed from every pore as she launched straight into him. Kodo accepted her right to anger. She hadn't been given all the facts but there was a reason for that.

'What do you mean he has Theo? How could you know that? How is that even possible? Theo wouldn't have just walked off by himself or with some stranger for that matter into some parallel world which probably doesn't even exist. Why would he do that? Why?' Her eyes were flashing and her body language said it all. She was mad and frustrated and a whole lot of other things besides. If Kodo were to be believed Theo was gone, taken by this Karalan. They couldn't bring him back, so why had Kodo brought her here? Why was he telling her about something they had no control over and why hadn't he told her the truth? What was the point exactly? Kodo's voice cut across her silent, verbal onslaught.

'The point exactly is, all I've told you is the truth and you're wrong about one thing. I do trust you. How could I not? As to why I never told you about Theo and Karalan, the simple fact was I couldn't. Once the decision had been made to bring you to Astaurias my main concern was to protect you and bring you here unharmed. I've held nothing else back from you. You must believe that. Theo has gone, but it doesn't mean we give up on him and not try to get him back. Oh and the reason by the way Arrianna that you're here is so that we can work something out to help us do just that. You can't do this alone. Theo was taken for a very specific reason. It'll be up to us to get him back from Karalan!' Kodo finished talking and stood patiently waiting for Arrianna's reaction. He hated seeing her anger and frustration. Not for the first time that day Arrianna was left feeling gauche and more than a little foolish. She still glared at Kodo, but it was a softened, less belligerent stare.

'How did you do that? How do you know what I'm thinking and what's going through my mind?' The question hung in the air. Arrianna looked quizzically at Kodo as the thought became a sudden realization. 'Tell me you're not telepathic, right?' She made it sound somehow like a challenge. She was willing him to deny it. The wind was taken out of her sails when he replied good-humouredly 'I am. Guilty as charged. One of the powers we all have, so from now on be very careful what you think! You never know who might be listening.'

The ice was broken. Arrianna accepted the truth about Theo and also the reasoning behind not telling her sooner. Now she had all the facts she felt frightened for him. Was he experiencing that same fear? The sickening response which came into her head was how could he be feeling anything else? He was out there somewhere on his own with strangers who would show him no love or give him any comfort. He'd be scared witless.

Arrianna's mind was awash with Star Beings, galaxies, portals, parallel worlds and Kodo's slightly less sensational by comparison, telepathic powers. She had been saturated with so much information it was difficult to concentrate on any one thing. What about herself? Did she have any powers she didn't know of? A little telepathic communication with Theo would really have lifted her spirits, but of course she realized the absurdity and futility of such wishful thinking. She didn't possess those powers. Her mind was still on Theo. Would they really be able to get him away from Karalan, and, how would they be able to achieve that? When this was over would she be able to leave Astaurias behind and return to her 'normal' life? Would she even want to?

Arrianna just wanted the questions to stop. She needed to know only what was going to happen next and she also needed to get out of the claustrophobic environment of the chamber. It was all beginning to close in on her and she didn't like it. She needed space and lots of it. Kodo was already way ahead in the thought stakes.

'We need to leave this chamber. It's time for you to see the bigger picture, time to meet your Star Family. Are you ready Arrianna?' He looked at her and saw the excitement mixed with a healthy apprehension bubble up inside her. There was no need for a reply. She stepped towards him and as she did so a large glistening archway opened up before her eyes. She focused on it and with Kodo alongside her she walked right through it.

Chapter 4

Arrianna thought a million stars must have rained down on top of her and covered her with stardust particles, for the light was spectacularly brilliant. She tried blinking to clear her vision and when that didn't work her hand came up to shield her eyes. There was no real need. They adjusted of their own accord. Arrianna was mesmerized. Like a laser show of rainbows, gigantic crystal prismic beams interspersed with miniature spiralling orbs of light too numerous to decipher, danced and spun through the air in a beautifully synchronized ballet. It was exquisite to watch. Every colour in the rainbow spectrum bounced of the other as each individual crystal created shimmering arcs of light which reflected and flitted across every available surface. It looked like all the crystals in the galaxies had united to create a crystal extravaganza. But nothing in Arrianna's life however, could have prepared her for the real sight beyond the archway. She had already run out of superlatives, and that was before any attempt had been made to describe the scene. Monumental didn't even begin to cover the sheer size and scale of the place they were in. It was stupendous, not just in its dimensions, but in the sensations it managed to evoke within her. This place stirred her senses like nothing else, and without having to think about it, she knew it had touched her soul. Kodo had been right. Every cell and every bone in her body felt it: a feeling of longing fulfilled and a sense of returning to her one true spiritual home. She felt her heart expand as she breathed in the love which reached out to enfold her with its soothing and calming embrace. It was a seminal moment and one she opened her heart to. Kodo was aware the very second the change in Arrianna's energy field took place. She looked so radiant and so beautiful at that moment, Kodo knew it would imprint itself in his psyche and he would remember it all his life. Something within his own heart was touched, releasing past emotions which he knew were better off left where they were. Buried. He tried to suppress the distant memory of just such a moment, only that time it had been on Earth, but images of Eleina still crept under the barriers he'd erected and came flooding back. Kodo couldn't look at Arrianna any more. It was too painful. A veil came down over his eyes and he turned his head away.

Arrianna's eyes darted from place to place trying to take it all in. It was an impossible task. At first she thought she and Kodo might be in some magnificent open-air cathedral of light, only this was a thousand times larger than any cathedral she'd ever seen before. There appeared to be no beginning or end to it and as she craned her neck to look upwards she saw it was exactly the same. The building reached up and stretched out into the nothingness she'd witnessed earlier in her chamber, and looked so precipitous it made her giddy. The internal structure was a feat of human engineering until Arrianna remembered where she was. Anything was possible here. Energy and the use of it could create any illusion. The void between her perception and star perception was infinite. She wondered if she would ever get used to it. Everywhere she looked she saw archways and alcoves, some with finely carved writings and strange metaphysical symbols, some as tall as two storey buildings. There were supports and columns as wide as the trunks of the largest oaks or giant redwoods. Level after level of construction. Liquid stairs and stairwells leading to walkways and chambers and interconnecting spaces. All centred around the vast, open quadrangle she and Kodo were standing in. She felt dwarfed by the magnitude of everything. Something was missing though. Then it finally hit her. There were no people.

It was almost as though an all-clear button had been pressed. The air came alive with the sound of laughter. Children's laughter. It was everywhere. That surprised Arrianna. For some reason she hadn't imagined there would be children living in Astaurias, but then again why shouldn't there be? The sound of running feet preceded tiny laughing faces as they came and peered out from behind the pillars and columns. Some were bolder than others and came quite close. Others who were less sure held back. There were so many of them, Arrianna was quite astounded. The majority were very young, but there were older ones too, an amazing mixture of boys and girls of many nationalities. Arrianna realised with a jolt they were like her. They weren't like Kodo at all. They were Earth Beings. She had no time to think of it further. Other voices joined in and drifted up and down and around her. Star Beings began to emerge to fill the walkways surrounding the quadrangle. There were hundreds, if not thousands of them and those were just the ones she could see around her. The whole length of the quadrangle as far as her eyes could focus filled with even more light from more Star Beings. Every single one she did make eye contact with, was just as magnificent as the next. It was an incredible sight. To have every eye in the place homed in and focused on her left Arrianna feeling quite unsettled and very conspicuous. She felt awkward and embarrassed and not at all sure she liked all the attention. She averted her eyes and turned to Kodo, seeking confirmation of a sort. To make herself heard she had to shout above the clamour and incoherent babble surrounding them.

'What am I supposed to do? Are they expecting me to say something or what?' Quite what she would have said she didn't really know. Kodo shook his head and shouted back.

'No. You're not expected to do a single thing. This is just our Star Beings way of welcoming you to our Ancient Halls. It's a special day for us. Just smile back and enjoy meeting your ancestors. There won't be too many moments in your life like this. Remember it well, Arrianna. Store it in your heart. When things quieten down a little I'll take you to the Sacred Star Chamber where you'll meet the Council. They're the ones who'll be working with you to get Theo back.' Arrianna suddenly remembered what she'd pushed to the back of her mind. She'd allowed herself some small respite from the agony of Theo's disappearance. She knew the same luxury had not been afforded to him. Theo was the only reason she had been able to experience Astaurias, and she felt guilty for forgetting that.

Kodo led Arrianna towards the Star Chamber and as they walked he explained a little about it.

'The Star Chamber is the most sacred of the chambers in our star group. It's the very heart of everything That Is, the place where the very first seeds of our star system was formed. It's from that sacred place that Star Beings are being sent to work against the forces of evil. From there we can oversee all star systems, not just our own. We also have eyes into other galaxies and universes. This is important because there are men out there who are jealous of Astaurias and would like to see it fail. We must be careful not to let that happen. The people whose job it is to protect Astaurias from attacks by rogue Beings or other infiltrators are called Gatekeepers. They're our first line of defence and not much has been known to slip through the force fields and grids they've put in place around our seven stars. They also protect the Inner Chamber when the Star Council presides. You already know our powers are immense but there is one thing above all others which must remain sacrosanct to us all. We must never abuse those powers. To do that would bring about the gravest repercussions and start the destruction of all that we believe in. Many have tried and for their efforts have been banished into a soulless, starless wilderness. If it's for the greater good we can intervene when another source asks us to do so, but every one of the Star Council must agree to this. Our powers allow us to travel through time at will and we can move in and out of time. It's the same when it comes to other dimensions; we have the ability to go there too. We can access other dimensions through our own sacred portals which are scattered right throughout your universe.

Kodo's step shortened as he came to a halt in front of an open doorway. There was nothing to differentiate it from all the others they had passed. If anything it was plainer by comparison. Arrianna could hear voices talking softly, though it was difficult to know what was being said. There was a pause then silence. She sensed a subtle change in Kodo. He was nervous and couldn't quite meet her enquiring look. He placed his hand in the small of her back and gently ushered her through into the chamber.

There was no opportunity to take in even the smallest detail of the chamber. Her eyes were riveted on the 'Mighty Being' walking with outstretched arms straight towards her. He was shorter than Kodo by a few inches but he was still an imposing figure. What he lacked in height was more than made up for in his stature and personality. He was broad and powerful for a man his age, and his hair was almost entirely white. His eyes were pale and long-lashed and his nose where it met with his brow had a small indentation from an accident with a stubborn fencing post. There was a small gap between his two lower front teeth which he'd insisted made him a good whistler even though he could never hold a tune. He had the bushiest eyebrows she'd ever seen and above and to the side of the right one a small dark mole. When he smiled at her, her world would come alive. Every line on his weather-beaten face told its own story and she knew most of them off by heart. Why wouldn't she? This man had been the pivotal force in both her own and Theo's life for the last several years. It was her grandfather.

The iciness started in the soles of Arrianna's feet and shot through her like a lightening rod. Her body felt clammy and tiny black spots began to cloud her vision. Grandfather caught her in his arms as she slumped unceremoniously to the ground.

Kodo's voice was far away but she heard it.

'You should have let me tell her Gaelun, right from the outset before she was even brought here. It might have been easier for her. It's one hell of a shock finding your recent departed is in her eyes at least alive and living another life she knows nothing of. How do you go about explaining that to her? How's that going to make her feel? What's that going to do to her?'

'Yes … what indeed?' Arrianna thought rather whimsically and abstractedly to herself. Kodo hadn't finished.

'You'll have to be careful how you handle her. She's been through so much. I've already been less than honest with her and she didn't like it one bit. She's not your granddaughter for nothing. She has a temper.' Kodo was upset and Gaelun knew it.

She was so cold. Her body and mind felt remote and oddly detached from each other. She was in that state between being conscious and total consciousness. Cold was banished as warmth crept up to overpower it. Her fingers began to tingle as wave after wave of energy began to clear the haziness in her mind.

'It's alright … she's coming round.' Were there ever five words spoken which sounded so wonderful? To hear that precious voice again made Arrianna want to cry. Her eyes opened and she scanned the familiar face looking for any sign that she'd got this all wrong. Inside her heart she knew she hadn't. Her arms came up to wrap themselves around his neck and as their energies merged she did cry. She didn't ever want to let him go. The words got stuck in the back of her throat and all she could manage to say was,

'Gaelun? … Grandfather?'

There was so much emotion, so much raw physical pain in Arrianna's voice, everyone was affected by it. Grandfather held her for a long, long time until she had no more tears left to shed. His words, when they came, were so very gentle and she loved him all the more for that. His strength became her strength until finally she removed her arms and parted from him. The love he felt for her shone from his eyes. For her part Arrianna couldn't take her eyes off him, not even for a second. Her hand reached out until it met his hand and he raised it to his cheek.

'My beautiful, sweet Arrianna ... how I've missed you.' Nothing further was said as they reacquainted themselves with the familial bonds which bound them. Kodo stood quietly observing.

Arrianna was still a little bewildered and confused. She distinctly remembered hearing more than one voice from inside the chamber, but Grandfather appeared to be on his own. What was even stranger still was that the chamber itself was entirely empty. No seats made from energy, no sign of anything at all; just a large empty space. She looked from Grandfather to Kodo and knew at once they were keeping something from her. There was still no sign of the Council. Where were they? Was it one of them she'd heard?

'Come and meet Wolf,' Grandfather said quite nonchalantly. 'I promise he won't bite. Well ... not you anyway. Not while we're here'. It was typical Grandfather humour. He roared that deep, resounding laugh which came from deep down in his sizeable belly. Then Kodo joined in. Friends reunited in a rare moment of joy.

The children concept Arrianna had accepted as soon as she set eyes on them, but animals, and wild ones at that, was definitely not something she would have expected to find, not right now, and certainly not in a chamber in the stars. Could things possibly get any stranger than they already were? A doorway appeared in front of all three of them, but before they even took one step towards it a wolf came padding through to stand beside Grandfather. It raised its nostrils to the air and looked straight at Arrianna. Only once before in her life had Arrianna seen a wolf at such close range and that had been in a wildlife sanctuary in the wildest regions of Canada. Her wolf was motherless and only weeks old and was being fed a bottle by hand. This was completely different. The wolf in the chamber was one of the most beautiful creatures she had ever seen. It was majestic in a way that only something wild could ever be: a natural born pack leader which stood head and shoulders above all else. For that reason alone, Arrianna was respectful of it. She never knew wolves could be that size and colour, and who would have imagined that an animal like a wolf would have such incredible burnt amber and gold coloured eyes? Then she remembered again for about the tenth time that day where she was. Arrianna wasn't so sure she wanted to get any closer. She kept what little distance there was between Wolf and herself. For some reason Kodo and Grandfather were still finding humour in the situation. She couldn't for the life of her think why.

'Wolf won't harm you, Arrianna. You're more likely to lick her to death aren't you, Wolf? Be nice now. Come and say hello!' Had Kodo completely lost the plot? In an instant she realized he probably had when she heard Wolf reply with some degree of smugness,

'She thinks I'm beautiful!' A look passed between Kodo and Grandfather. The consternation on Arrianna's face was almost amusing. She stared at them both.

'Tell me I didn't hear that. He spoke. Wolf spoke, didn't he?' The dawning realization that her mind had registered the words set off a whole different train of thought. If everyone had heard it including herself, was it a sign that she was beginning to access powers of her own? Was that even possible?

'You didn't imagine anything, Arrianna,' Grandfather said. 'You're becoming aware of a new power, that's all.' He said it so matter-of-factly but to Arrianna this was huge.

Was this something she'd always have from now on? Would even more powers be revealed to her? There were so many things she just did not know.

'You're telepathic, just as we are, just as Wolf is. It's one of several powers Wolf has and it's his way of communicating. It's a special gift, and a very useful tool at times. Just remember, everyone here has it. When the children you saw are old enough, they'll have it too. Now, come and meet Wolf properly. You're going to be seeing a lot of him.' Arrianna had no option. She decided bravery was a better option than her initial fear. With a confidence she didn't realise she possessed she walked over and got down on her knees until she was level with Wolf. She steadied her shaking hand and let her fingers sink deep into his long luxuriant coat. It was so soft and warm and she wanted to bury her face in it, but didn't dare. She wasn't that courageous. Not yet anyway. Wolf made it easy for her. He did exactly what Kodo said he would do. His tongue lolled out and made contact with her skin. It felt coarse and wet and very long. He licked her hands, he licked her face, and then he allowed Arrianna to play with his thick golden-tipped ears. It didn't stop there. Wolf was enjoying himself. He manoeuvred his body right up against hers and rolled over to allow her to feel his strong, gangly legs and his large supple paws. Arrianna almost toppled over with the sheer weight of him. He was bestowing a special privilege on Arrianna, something which only a very few were ever granted. By making himself vulnerable and exposing his under belly like that he was effectively letting her know that he trusted her. It was another special moment in a day full of just such moments.

Arrianna went through two further antechambers before they reached the inner Star Chamber. All conversation ceased as Grandfather led them into the chamber. Heads turned in recognition, then conversations were resumed once more. Arrianna counted at least twenty Star Beings in the chamber but no introductions were forthcoming. No council members here then, she thought to herself. She turned sideways and glanced at Kodo. He grinned back, tapped the side of his head and mouthed, 'Remember'.

The chamber was amazing. It felt as though someone had taken one single room and placed it right in the middle of space. Arrianna was reminded of the triangle which had transported her to Astaurias but there all comparisons ended. This domed room of light was vast. She had that same sensation of wanting to reach out and touch. As she looked about her she realized why it had been named the Star Chamber. Taking up the greater part of the circular space was a massive, pale aqua crystal star which was deeply embedded into the floor. The energy emanating from it was phenomenal. A couple of hundred people could have stood on it and still there would be space left over. The rest of the chamber was a hive of concentration. It looked to be the futuristic communications centre it was. Star Beings, some individually, others in groups, worked with instruments which she presumed gave information on planetary positionings. Strange machines of highly advanced technology whirred and flashed out melodious waves of sound. There were charts everywhere and again she was overwhelmed by the magnitude of such an operation. She looked out into space as enormous, oddly shaped bands of trapped particles and long lines of strung out rocks and inter stellar dust floated past en route to deeper space. Nothing was still. Swirling clouds of debris and columns like tornadoes, bruised and buffeted existing star fields on an endless celestial pathway. Whether by chance or not, Arrianna saw not one but two shooting stars. That was a sign of good news to come, her mother had always said. She certainly hoped so. A young man and woman about her own age stepped away from the other Star Beings and came to stand alongside Kodo. The man reminded Arrianna a little of her father with his dark straight hair and fine bone structure, and the girl when she turned to face Arrianna had the most beautiful smooth, coffee coloured skin and dark, almost black, penetrating eyes. Grandfather introduced them as Nikolai and Yula. He explained they were both Gatekeepers and they would stay with the group for a while. Arrianna had never heard the name Yula before and wondered where she might be from. 'Peru,' came the girl's telepathic response. Arrianna looked at her and her eyes had softened and there was a hint of a smile in them. She felt Wolf's soft muzzle brush against her hand and was reassured by the comforting contact.

Everything happened so quickly after that. Invisible walls came down inside the chamber separating everyone in the group from the other Star Beings. The chamber was effectively closed off. The star in the centre of the chamber's floor rose marginally from the ground and as its points opened slowly outwards it revealed six people. The Star Council had finally arrived.

Chapter 5

There was a tremendous sense of anticipation and purpose in the air, a moment of pure theatre in a stage set to impress. Arrianna watched closely as the Star Council made their entrance. For her at least, it was a definitive debut performance. It was abundantly apparent why Kodo had been so descriptive in his praise of them. She hadn't known what to expect but 'Mightiest' more than adequately covered the select group of Star Beings standing before her. When she'd first heard Kodo use that term, Arrianna had conjured up images in her head of the wonderful mythical Beings Grandfather had brought so vividly to life in the tales of her childhood. He'd once described Beings from Sirius who were so mighty and so tall their heads could touch her bedroom ceiling. Memories of those times came back. She could remember quite clearly sitting in total awe and endless fascination as night after night Grandfather had worked his magic with fantasy characters fighting off impossible foes in improbable destinations. After the events of today, it was becoming obvious to Arrianna that perhaps they hadn't been so mythical after all. Grandfather definitely deserved plaudits for his efforts. She realized how clever he had been. Not quite all the truth, but not all lies either. She adored him, but on this occasion she felt aggrieved and more than a little cheated. He was such a special part of her life but she didn't really know him at all. If it hadn't been for Theo, she would never have known the real truth.

The Council were quite unique in a way other Star Beings were not. It wasn't solely their physical aspects Arrianna had difficulty putting into words. They combined assuredness with an almost regal air, an impression that alluded to them being a part of something far greater. Acute awareness belied their apparent stillness. The clear golden auras around them were unlike anything she'd seen so far. As they moved they shimmered and their auras intensified. Arrianna knew their vibration was at a higher level than any other person in the chamber. It was their indefinable sense of presence and all-knowingness which made it impossible for Arrianna to look away. Grandfather was the first to step forward. When he joined them, his vibration rose as he took on his mantle of being one of the Mightiest. A column of intense white light rose up and spread out across the chamber as the power of seven were united. Every nerve ending in Arrianna's body came alive with the energy it generated. She felt blessed with the love of the seven and was thankful for it. Grandfather had told her they were the 'Keepers of the Light' and 'Guardians of the Eternal Flame' which burned deep in the Celestial Mountains she'd looked down upon. Arrianna had little or no conception of such things and what that meant. The responsibilities of the seven seemed onerous and even mightier than themselves.

Grandfather decided to get things underway by suggesting everyone present move to sit around a crystal table which had miraculously appeared from nowhere. As she walked across the chamber Arrianna had time to study the seven more closely. Excluding Grandfather, there were four men and two women. Two of the men were tall, like Kodo. Another was about Grandfather's height, only a lot thinner, and the fourth one was small and slight in demeanour. As with many Star Beings it was impossible to guess their ages. It was the same with the women. One looked to be in her mid thirties, the other slightly older. Either one of them could just as easily have been as old as the millennium itself. Both were breathtaking and wonderfully exotic, but it was to the younger of the two Arrianna's eyes were drawn. She had a short, feathery cap of silver hair which rested delicately upon her beautiful sculptured head. Her eyes were wide and almond shaped and the colour of burnished gold. Where her third eye was, a small crystal star glittered. She looked like some mysterious warrior princess, only dressed in floating white robes. On her index finger she wore a long oval ring carved from the same pale aqua crystal as the star she'd emerged from. On her other outstretched hand there rested a beautiful white hawk. Arrianna couldn't help herself; she stared quite openly at them both. Grandfather came over and gently stroked the hawk. A small frisson of something passed between the woman and himself.

'Had they been lovers at one time?' immediately came into Arrianna's mind. Where had that come from? She was a little shocked that she'd even thought that, but even more mortified when she knew that of course the woman had heard her. Grandfather just chuckled to himself.

'Lady Samia, this is my granddaughter Arrianna.' She smiled to reveal white, even teeth. Her voice was strong and humour ran right through it. There was a glint in her eye as she half turned to respond to Grandfather.

'It's all right, Gaelun. Everyone here knows who Arrianna is. She's just as beautiful as I'd imagined her to be.' She looked straight into Arrianna's eyes and reached out her bejewelled hand to touch her tenderly on the cheek. 'Welcome Arrianna. Welcome to our home in the stars.' Each Star Being in turn came forward to introduce themself, but there was little time for lengthy social pleasantries. That wasn't on the agenda.

All eleven finally settled themselves around the table. They fell silent when Grandfather raised his hand to bring the meeting to order. The playfulness he'd had in his voice was gone, replaced by a more serious tone. He directed his words to no one specific person.

'You all know why we're here and why Arrianna has been brought to Astaurias. You're also aware that you've been privileged to information which she has not. Firstly, I'll ask Kodo to bring you up to date with what new information he's obtained about my grandson's abduction because that is exactly what it was, an abduction to get back at me for Karalan's banishment into the wilderness as he sees it. Arrianna then needs to be told the exact nature of what we're facing and the forces we're up against.'

Arrianna watched and listened as Kodo began the task of updating everyone. Talk of abduction made her uneasy. The nervous feeling in her stomach returned. It was no easier for her having to hear it the second time round.

'The Watchers have definitely taken Theo, but the bad news from our point of view is they've moved him on deep into the heart of Skerrilorn. My informants tell me there are also several hundred forgotten ones in the particular holding place where Theo is. It's not going to be easy to get him away. Even if we could, how are we going to get the others out? I think Karalan would notice a mass exodus like that, don't you? His Watchers are everywhere. Nothing takes place in Skerrilorn that he doesn't know about. There's another very real problem. The ones he has managed to turn will not come voluntarily. We've got to think about that and decide what we need to do. I know our priority is Theo but the others cannot be left behind.'

It was the first time Karalan's parallel universe had been named and the first time Arrianna had heard of the 'forgotten ones'. This was something altogether new. Who were they? She didn't fully understand. The impression she was under was that it was just Theo. Wolf chose that moment to sidle up against her chair and place his head in her lap. She found her courage once more and with that her voice.

'I know the Watchers have taken Theo, but who are the forgotten ones and what is the holding place? Why would there be such a place? What's its purpose? None of this makes a whole lot of sense to me.' Arrianna paused then decided to just go ahead and say exactly what her instincts were telling her. 'You're holding something back, I know. What is it? Why don't you just tell me and get it over with?' The frustration Arrianna felt was plain for all to see. Her eyes scanned the table, waiting for someone, anyone, to tell her the truth. What use were her telepathic powers if no one was giving anything away? There was a moment's hesitation. One of the taller Star Beings who was called Tamu, and whom Arrianna had liked instantly because of his bright, smiling face, returned her gaze and held it. Before one word was spoken Arrianna knew it was going to be bad. His blue eyes were troubled and his expression was grim. He tried hard not to show his anger but had too much respect for this beautiful, intelligent Earth Being not to tell her the absolute truth. He directed his words directly at her.

'Arrianna, Gaelun has asked us all to be brief and this I will try to do. Everyone around this table has their own story of Karalan to tell you and before you leave Astaurias you will hear every single one of them. Over and above our work in the stars we each have a section of your planet Earth to watch over.' He turned and acknowledged the Star Being with the slight demeanour. 'Amaron and myself look over the Americas, North and South and also the Poles. Our responsibilities specifically entail the protection of all children from the very young up until they can be independent in their own rights. Race and religion don't ever come into it. It's a harsh reality of life, Arrianna, but there are millions of children out there around the world who have no one to look after them. No homes to live in, no food to eat, no one to protect them. Their hearts beat but no one knows or wants to know they exist. They have no voice and no one to speak out on their behalf. There is such disparity and much despair amongst the children of the nations. Many must fend for themselves and try to survive as best they can. For the best part we watch over them without direct intervention. So many dreadful things are going on in your world that you are unaware of. Children are abducted every minute of the day. Children are killed and no one even notices. Moral conscience is a thing of the past to a lot of people for whatever reason. Don't get me wrong, the majority of people are good and they do care, but many children still slip through the net. These are children the society of the world forgot. We cannot help them all, but those we can, we do. When all seems lost for them, we bring them home to the stars just as we've always done throughout the ages. Centuries ago it might have been through the onslaught of the Conquistadors or invading armies, today it's probably through neglect or poverty. Yula here was once such child. She was one of the street children in Peru. All day long she lived in the sewers beneath the streets and only at night could she come out and steal the food which would keep her alive. All hope had gone for her and we only just got to her in time.'

Arrianna was shocked, really shocked. She felt enormous guilt. Had she–? Telepathy from Kodo stopped her mind from going further.

'Don't Arrianna. It is a wasted emotion.' He made it sound so cold and clinical. She looked at him but he was looking at Yula.

Lady Merissa took up where Tamu had left off. She had a leonine quality to her and was just as breathtaking as Arrianna had first thought. Her hair was silky and golden and fell in thick loose waves down about her shoulders. The only pieces of ornamentation she wore were a single star around her neck and a ring of stars around her crown. Both looked exactly the same as Lady Samia's crystals. They sparkled and glistened with each gentle movement of her lithe, supple frame. Her skin was pale and translucent and her eyes were the colour of the stars she wore. When she spoke her voice was gentle and had an enchanting lilt to it.

'The children whose countries we look over are each taken to the star of the Star Being responsible for them. For me that is Europe and the Russias. All of our seven stars take care of the children. They need to feel safe so they can explore and grow and reach their full potential. We nurture them and protect them and when they are grown, they are given a choice. They can live out their lives in the stars or they can return to Earth to fulfil their desires and ambitions. Many choose another path. They dedicate their lives to the stars but can return to Earth for short periods of time to help in the rescue of the forgotten ones. We're one of the closest star systems to Earth, so it's easier for us than most. Time means very little here. When your time comes Arrianna, you'll be able to return to Earth before anyone even notices you're gone.' The words only brought home to Arrianna how ignorant she was when it came to knowledge of such things.

Johai was tall with clearly defined muscles in his neck and shoulders and far more powerful than Arrianna had originally thought. His features made her think he could easily have been a wrestler with his shaven head and enormous squared-off fingers. His area of protection stretched from the Middle East to the Pacific Rim. There was a fluidity in the way he moved his body which made him appear more athletic than the others. A silly thought came into her head, but in the end she resisted the temptation to reach out and touch the shiny smoothness of his head. Everyone around the table smiled and Yula giggled. Arrianna felt herself blush and she turned her attention to her hands. Johai started to speak.

'Whether it was coincidence or not we'll never really know, but around the time your parents drowned Arrianna and Gaelun took over your upbringing, several things started to happen to children all around the world. It wasn't just the forgotten ones who were affected. Children from families were also being targeted. At first we thought it might just be a glitch in the numbers, but there was more to it than that. We began to realize that large pockets of children were disappearing. The dispossessed were vanishing. Gaelun was more or less Earthbound bringing you and Theo up. He couldn't just pack up and go off on his journeys as he once used to. There were times when he managed to get back here, but they were too few. We needed his wisdom and leadership to enforce the power of seven, but you and Theo needed him too. Kodo was able to visit often and through him Gaelun kept things going as best he could. I think we all knew even then it was never going to be enough.' Johai stopped talking. Something clicked in Arrianna's mind. Certain recollections of instances began to fall into place. If ever there was a true 'light bulb' moment then it was now. She knew it was just the reaction to what she'd heard about Grandfather, but nonetheless, she still felt a sense of betrayal. It was completely irrational. What else could he have done? He certainly couldn't have told them about Astaurias. He was torn between two directions and she and Theo had been the ones he'd stayed to love and look after.

Arrianna began to wonder when Phoenix, the last Star Being, would interject. Her telepathy must have kicked in. He was the quietest of all seven; a man of very few words and she had no idea at all what to make of him. Lady Samia looked after the African Continent so he must look after Australasia. He didn't have the look of having risen from any ashes; in fact he appeared to be the most ordinary of all the Star Beings. Therein Arrianna suspected lay his greatest strength. Because of that she instinctively knew he was probably the most dangerous. His voice was clear and turned out to be the softest of all. Arrianna was thankful he was on her side and she didn't have to consider him as an adversary.

'Five or six months ago events very nearly overtook us. A critical moment was reached. We found out from some of our Star Beings who'd secretly entered Skerrilorn that Karalan was responsible for the disappearances of the children. He and his Watchers are like phantoms in the night. They flit between worlds with impunity. They're in and out so quickly it's difficult, almost impossible to spot them. Anyway, Karalan was abducting these children and holding them in special units or places until such time as they could be turned. A form of mass indoctrination if you like then takes place. There are other Beings out there whom we call Slakers, and they are the ones Karalan has recruited for that specific task. They were once soldiers of fortune but now they inhabit the darkest, bleakest spots in the world. Evil and cruelty have taken over their lives and it is they Karalan has given the job to of turning the children. Children's minds are poisoned against their own kind, and what little love they have inside them is killed. They are encouraged to explore their dark side and taught to love that darkness. The Slakers fill their minds with all that is Dark. It takes no time for impressionable young minds to be swayed. Those who won't be turned are kept until they do. Only then are they released.

Violence and aggression become the diktats of the day. Once their minds have been successfully wiped of all that is good, the majority of the children are returned to Earth to spread their violence and misery. The forgotten ones roam the streets, very often in packs, seeking to inflict their own brand of evil justice. The so-called lucky parents are reunited with children they no longer know. They are faced with out of control children who have no love in their hearts. The children's sole aim is Karalan's aim. He seeks havoc and destruction, but above all he seeks total power. To be able to turn Gaelun's grandson over to The Dark gives him pleasure. He's never truly forgiven Gaelun for his banishment. Word has it he will train Theo as he would his heir to work alongside him. It doesn't stop there either. In his poor, deluded mind he won't be content with the powers he proposes to take on Earth. He believes he can corrupt and take over Astaurias. We reached a point three months ago when everything hung in the balance.

Karalan's evil was beginning to overtake the Powers of Good. Something had to be done to reverse that. We needed Gaelun back. Even though he'd chosen this lifetime on Earth, the greater good could only be served by his return to Astaurias.'

At first Arrianna wasn't sure she'd heard him properly. When she looked around the faces at the table, she knew she had. She was slow. It took several seconds for the implications of Phoenix's words to sear her brain. And sear it they did. She did not believe him. How could she? She was completely dumbstruck. They'd finally come round to telling her. She was now privileged to the same privileged information as the council. It was funny, it didn't make her feel in the least way privileged. To have accepted that would have meant that Grandfather knew he was going to die. Someone was suffering an amnesia bypass or from selective memory syndrome and Arrianna knew it wasn't her. Grandfather died in his sleep. That was the way it had been. Hell, she was the one who'd found his lifeless form propped up against his pillows when he failed to appear at breakfast. Now the clarity of those perceptions of that dreadful day so deeply ingrained in her mind were being rewritten? Arrianne didn't know what to believe. He wouldn't knowingly have left herself and Theo, would he? Somehow, though in reality she had no idea just how, he could have prepared them for their impending loss couldn't he? And the Council? Phoenix had said it was for the greater good. Arrianna's mind debated which was the greater good, but in her heart she already knew. It didn't make it any easier for her to accept. Another dilemma presented itself. Had the Star Council actually played a part in Grandfather's death on Earth? Did they really have the powers to call him back? It was a non-question and the answer was, of course, they had.

Arrianna listened to the silence in the chamber. She knew every single eye was fixed on her. What were they all waiting for? Did they expect her to stamp her feet like a petulant child at the unfairness of it all? The truth was she didn't know what to think any more. All ties with her emotions and her senses had been severed and she felt nothing inside. Wolf lifted his head and started to gently lick the back of her hand. She wanted to cry. Wolf can comfort me but my own grandfather can't. She caught his eye and neither looked away. It was left to Lady Samia to call a halt to the proceedings. Sitting to the right of Arrianna, she had said very little throughout the entire discourse.

'I think Arrianna needs a break Gaelun. It's been a long day for her and she's had one shock after another. She needs a little time.' She made light of it, but it almost sounded like a gentle rebuke. As if on cue, Arrianna's stomach rumbled. The last time she'd eaten was the previous evening. 'Besides,' Lady Samia continued, 'your granddaughter's stomach is complaining. She's hungry Gaelun. We can finish off after she's had something more substantial than fresh air to feed off.'

Arrianna thanked her in her mind. She knew she had found a wonderful ally.

'Will you be my ally too?' she silently asked the beautiful hawk on Lady Samia's hand.

'I will' came the even more beautiful response.

Chapter 6

As the group around the table either got up or continued to sit and talk amongst themselves, Yula rose and came towards Arrianna. She led her to the far side of the chamber, where once again energy had created a small circular table.

'What would you like to eat Arrianna?' The table in front of her was bare. Her eyebrows raised in query.

'I don't really know. What is there to eat, Yula?' It was like a game of cat and mouse. Arrianna knew she wasn't the cat. She felt she was being gently toyed with by Yula, but she didn't mind. There was no malice in her voice, only kindness.

'Think of something you'd like to eat and you will have it … anything.' Okay, Arrianna thought. I'll go along with this and see where it takes us. She imagined large bowls of delicious fruits and as an afterthought a mug of her favourite hot chocolate. Everything materialized instantly before her. She reached out to see if it was all real. It was.

'Wow … that was amazing. How did you do that, Yula?' Arrianna turned and glanced sideways in her direction.

'I didn't Arrianna. You did. You thought it, and it became your instant manifestation. That's how it happens in Astaurias. It's wonderful isn't it?' They looked at each other and laughed out loud.

The atmosphere in the room had lightened a little with the break, but as they all came together again, everyone knew that wouldn't last. Arrianna had reached a place of truce in her heart about her grandfather. She walked purposefully towards him and took her place at his side. Beneath the table she reached out for his hand. It was a moment of reconciliation. They both knew it. Nothing further was needed.

The discussions went on well into what Arrianna felt sure must be night. No firm resolutions had been made. The enormity of what they would have to undertake was staggering.

'Karalan is not an altogether stupid man. We wouldn't be faced with all this if he was.' Everyone listened intently as Kodo spoke. His voice was calm but Arrianna could see steel in his eyes.

'He's not just sitting waiting for some response from us. He's expecting us to go into Skerrilorn. He wants us to make a move and we will, but it must be on our terms when we're ready. We know where his portals are throughout his universe. That's not the problem. We can access them and get through them, but doing it in such a way that his radar won't pick up is definitely a major stumbling block for us. We just cannot move the tens of thousands of Star Beings needed into Skerrilorn undetected. The Watchers and Slakers wouldn't pay much attention to a few small groups filtering through but anything larger than that we can just forget. We have to use the portals. There's no way around it.' The chamber was silent once more. Arrianna knew everyone's thought process was anything but silent.

Johai spoke. 'Everything Kodo has said so far is true. We need to be cleverer than Karalan and come up with the unexpected. If we try to move in with force we will achieve nothing. We'll be defeated before we've even begun. You've heard the old saying about using a sledgehammer to crack a nut. We must be subtle and not forceful. Karalan will expect force but we shall not give it to him. What we need is something small and undetectable, something which can be transported or small enough to be carried by a team leader in a box. Something which will weigh very little going through a portal.' There was almost an air of mischief about Johai when he asked what he already knew. 'Any ideas anyone?' It took all of one second for the penny to drop, then another, then another.

'Excellent!' said Phoenix.

'Brilliant!' said Amaron. There was a buzz of excitement around the table. Had she missed something? Everyone was congratulating Johai, but what for? Arrianna was the only one in the chamber who hadn't got it. Grandfather squeezed her hand and spoke to her.

'Johai is talking about winged insects, Arrianna. What he's proposing is that because of the numbers of Star Beings involved they must use their powers to shape-shift into insects. Once they're through the portals, whoever the chosen leaders are can release them at intervals or when they reach their destinations. It just depends on the circumstances at the time. The insects can stay as they are or shape-shift back into Star Beings. They'll be disguised to blend in and they'll be able to spread out silently and quickly. That's what we need, the element of surprise. Hopefully it will help us gain an advantage and the upper hand.' For once Arrianna knew what Grandfather meant by shape-shifting. She'd read a book on South American shamanism where one of the shamans from the Yanomami tribe had become one with a jaguar. People might have thought it improbable, but the book was so beautifully expressed and written with such clarity and insight, she believed it. Johai's idea was clever but Arrianna still had questions.

'How are insects going to be able to help the children? How will they be able to deal with the Watchers and Slakers?' As was turning out to be the norm, she felt she was at least fifty steps behind everyone else. They had already worked it out but she had not. It needed to be explained to her. Lady Samia answered her questions.

'Before each Star Being departs from the Star System they will be given a crystal to carry. Each crystal will come from our Celestial Mountains, and each will hold a spark from the Eternal Flame. When the Star Beings shape-shift, the crystals will also shape-shift. They will become miniscule. This however will not lessen the power of the crystals. One simple touch from a crystal will instantly banish The Darkness from the children's hearts. They will immediately be filled with love again and their minds will be brought into the light once more. People from Earth will not be able to accept or understand this, but for us this act of healing is normal. It really does happen as quickly as that and that is what the Star Beings and insects must try to do. They must reach the children and touch their hearts. I make it sound easy, but in reality it won't be that simple to get to the children. There will be a lot to overcome. Apart from the Slakers there is Karalan himself. So many who surround him are Star Beings who have gone over to The Dark side. Like him they still have certain powers. Know in your heart Arrianna that ours are greater. For that reason We cannot leave Astaurias. The power of seven must remain united here. You will have as much assistance as we can give you. You will not be alone. One thing you must all be aware of is there is not a lot of natural light left on Skerrilorn. Karalan has lived there so long his universe has almost become a reflection of himself. It is a dark, foreboding place, where people live in the shadows, and little survives. There is no beauty of any description in that God-forsaken place. There is one further thing to think about. We know Karalan holds the forgotten ones close to the portals, but his universe is large. It will still mean it could easily take a day or longer to reach the holding places. We won't be able to slip in, do what must be done, then slip back out again. We must use the remaining hours of the night wisely. Every detail must be thought out beforehand. Everything should be coordinated so that all the portals in Karalan's universe are accessed at the same time. It's also important you know just what long, uncharted distances will be involved, and remember, when it's over, we still have to take the children to the portals and get them safely through to the other side. Many of them would have been weakened even before they were taken. After their experiences on Skerrilorn many will be damaged further. The crystals will do what they were chosen to do, but, all the Star Beings must use all their own healing powers to help those most in need. Whatever happens to the children after they are brought back, Lady Merissa and myself will be responsible for. What we cannot hope to address at this precise moment are the ones already released back to Earth by Karalan. That will have to be worked on. Out of the ones we do manage to release, some may be able to be left, but I imagine many will be brought back to Astaurias. We'll never have had such a massive influx, but it must be done. The children have suffered enough. They must know peace.' Lady Samia turned towards Kodo. His gaze was unswerving. 'Kodo, you will lead a small advance party into Skerrilorn. We've already been told Theo is being held much further away than most of the holding places. We're relieving Nikolai and Yula from their Gatekeeper duties to accompany you.' There was a long pause. Arrianna was waiting. 'And ... and,' her head demanded. The delay was interminable and the silence deafening as she studied the impassive faces of those around her. A sensation akin to panic rose up inside her. She had to go! They couldn't leave her out now could they? She searched Grandfather's face looking for confirmation but seeing none. Her mind was defying him to say no. 'Don't do this to me. Please. I can't be left behind.' For a split second a strange haunted look flirted with Grandfather's eyes. He let out a sigh and gave a brief, short nod in Lady Samia's direction. A message passed between the two though in reality everyone sitting around the table understood the implications of that nod and just how much it had cost Gaelun.

'You've made the right decision, Gaelun. She must fulfil her destiny.' She smiled at Arrianna. 'And of course Arrianna will also accompany you Kodo. You must take great care of her. She does not have all the powers you possess. We will do our best to give her protection before you all leave, but remember you must be vigilant at all times. Be careful of Karalan. He plays games with people's minds. Expect the unexpected and trust only each other. You are there for one single purpose: Theo and the forgotten ones. It will be up to the four of you to find them.' Lady Samia saw the look of apprehension on Arrianna's face. 'Don't worry. Others won't be that far behind you. They can cover long distances. They'll soon catch up with you.'

Everything that needed to be said had been said. A decision had been reached. Lady Samia faced the group. 'Are we all agreed we proceed with the plan we have put forward?' Every single head in the chamber nodded in agreement and relief. The group disbanded as everyone rose from the table. It had been a long night. Arrianna felt her energy sap. She was wiped out. Kodo came towards Grandfather and herself. He walked with purpose now and Arrianna noticed there was a determination about the set of his mouth. He was a man on a mission.

'Gaelun, there is a lot to do and one hell of a lot to prepare before we can leave. I'll take Nikolai and Yula with me now and we'll set the wheels in motion. We can meet up later for any last minute instructions if that's all right with you?' He wasn't really asking permission. It was a declaration rather than a question. When he turned to Arrianna his face had softened and there was a look, a something in his eyes she'd never seen before. 'I'm glad you're coming with us, Arrianna. The team wouldn't be complete without you.' She wondered if he was having fun at her expense with the humour which ran through his voice. But he wasn't. He seemed genuinely pleased. 'Before we go, though, you must rest your body and mind for a while. You will need all the energies you possess to get through the coming days. Don't fret. The morning will come soon enough. For tonight it's best you stay here with your grandfather. I'll see you when you wake up, okay?' All the strain and uncertainty had been removed from his face as he spoke to her. He was almost like Kodo of old. He bent down and patted Wolf on the head. Before Arrianna could respond, Kodo turned around and with a nod in the general direction of the Council, he, Nikolai and Yula disappeared swiftly through the door of the Star Chamber.

The remaining Star Council were showing signs of making a move also, but they held back. Arrianna and Grandfather moved across the chamber to join them. Both Lady Samia and Lady Merissa broke off their conversations as they approached. Hints of smiles played around their lips. Amaron was talking animatedly to Phoenix. Johai and Tamu were seated again. Neither was speaking. Both appeared lost in their own thoughts. They broke off from whatever those thoughts had been and looked up.

'Well, Gaelun,' Johai spoke as he uncurled his long frame and stood up. He walked around the table. He was speaking to Grandfather but it was meant for everyone. 'So it begins. No turning back now.' The tone of his voice only emphasized what they were all thinking. There could be no denying the enormity and seriousness of what lay ahead. No one could take this lightly. Arrianna sensed the weariness in Grandfather's stance. He looked round them all and replied sombrely, 'No, no going back. Not this time.' A heavy, ominous feeling crept up and over into Arrianna's heart. Now that the decision had been made she didn't mind admitting to herself that she was frightened. So much could go wrong and she didn't want to let anyone down, especially Theo or Grandfather. It was really scary thinking what the Slakers were like, what Karalan was like and what he was capable of. Because she was so tired, she allowed the doubts to sneak in. They started to multiply and fill her mind.

Lady Merissa placed her hand on Arrianna's arm. 'Don't Arrianna. Don't think dark thoughts. You're only buying into the fear if you do that. Have faith in yourself and faith in the Star Beings. Karalan will be defeated. Light will prevail. His darkness will not win the day.' Arrianna was quite mesmerized with the intensity and conviction in Lady Merissa's eyes. She could have hugged her at that moment. Instead, she placed her free hand on top of Lady Merissa's and thanked her. Phoenix approached Arrianna. She found herself still being a little on guard. It was silly to feel that way, after all they were both on the same side, but, she couldn't help herself. There was just something about him which made it impossible for her to feel relaxed around him. 'What now?' she wondered as he stood directly in front of her. Phoenix seemed to sense her uncertainty and did his best to put her at ease. There was a wry, almost amused look on his face.

'It's all right. You can relax. Nothing awful is going to happen to you! We just have a couple of things we'd like to show you before you leave to go to Skerrilorn. We want you to know that if at any time you need to call upon any one of us for help, we will send you that help. Of course, you understand we cannot come to you in person because we must remain here, but our power animals can come to your assistance. You already know Gaelun has Wolf and he has many special powers. So does Lady Samia's Hawk. We'd like you to meet all the power animals you can call upon. For practical reasons which will become apparent, it was not thought to be in your best interest to bring two of the animals. Suffice to say, just as Tamu and Amaron share regions in the Universe, so they share an animal – a black panther to be precise. For Johai, his pride and joy is a black bear, simply called Bear. The sole reason I'm telling you this you understand, is in case you ever do need to call either or both, you won't have any problem recognizing them.' It was Phoenix's strange way of trying to be funny and make light of it. Arrianna could not suppress her laughter. She was beginning to feel more relaxed around him. In fact, she was beginning to like him.

'Come and meet Snake. I think you'll like him. He's my power animal.' He led her over to a large energy basket. Inside lay a magnificent gold and white striped snake. Arrianna's breathing slowed as she weighed up her next move. Calmly and deliberately she bent down and carefully picked him up. He wasn't a very large snake, but he felt heavy for his size. His body was dry and warm. She stroked his underbelly which he seemed to like. He didn't recoil. Phoenix was surprised. He hadn't expected that reaction. Most people would have run a mile at the sight of a snake, but Arrianna hadn't. Then Phoenix began to realize something. She had handled snakes before. She liked them. Gaelun laughed out loud at the look on Phoenix's face.

'Phoenix, my granddaughter spent four years of her life in East Africa. She has no fear of snakes and certainly not one whose belly she can stroke.' Phoenix's eyebrows rose as he said what was so clearly obvious to him now.

'Ah, yes, of course.' He smiled almost sheepishly back at Gaelun, but when he looked at Arrianna his eyes were laughing and kind. Arrianna eased Snake back into the basket where he wrapped himself around it. His tongue flicked out constantly, all the time searching for any vibration in the air. His eyes remained open and alert, conscious of every movement around him. Grandfather might have joked about snakes, but Arrianna was acutely aware that Snake was no ordinary reptile. He could be a dangerous opponent and they all knew it.

Lady Merissa was next. She took Arrianna over to a gnarled old energy branch. Sitting preening herself and cleaning her feathers was what Arrianna thought was a crow, only it wasn't. Lady Merissa leant forward and gently stroked the breast feathers of the bird.

'This is Raven. Not only is she very wise but she's also rather beautiful, don't you think?' Wolf chose that moment to amble over and inspect the other 'beautiful' animal in the chamber. Raven let out a loud 'Caw,' flapped her wings and moved to a higher branch, taking her vanity with her. She looked down on Wolf with an air of calculated disinterest. Arrianna thought it really amusing.

Tamu leant over Arrianna's shoulder and spoke to Lady Merissa.

'I hate to break this up but we have our work to do. The hours left are short and we still have to go to the Celestial Mountains. We should leave now if we're to get back in time for the Star Beings' leaving.' Everyone agreed. A feeling of urgency had returned to spur them on. The time for farewells had come round so quickly. In the short time Arrianna had known these Magnificent Beings, she'd not only benefited from their power and their wisdom, she'd also been a recipient of their copious love and spirit. She had been doubly blessed. She almost wished they could have stayed a little longer, but it would not have been possible. Each of them must go. That thought brought home the realization that very shortly she'd be saying another farewell. She had no idea how she was going to cope with that parting.

One by one 'The Mightiest' came forward. Tamu and Amaron were the first. Whenever she would think of them again, they would always be together. She liked that.

Johai, he of the shiny head, was next. The expression was sombre and there were no smiles from him. His voice was dulled and the words few.

'Be safe, Arrianna.'

Phoenix said nothing. He placed his hand on her crown, let his energy flow through her, then turned on his heel and walked away. Lady Merissa came and stood beside Arrianna. She lifted Arrianna's hand and placed it on her heart.

'Be strong, Arrianna. Remember we are with you.' With a beautiful wide smile and a small inclination of her head she stepped away and joined the others in the centre of the star. Arrianna found it difficult to look at Lady Samia and Hawk as they approached her. It was all a little overwhelming for her. She stroked Hawk for the first and last time. She'd expected a speech from Lady Samia, but she'd leant forward and kissed her softly on the cheek.

'Don't forget us Arrianna. Be gentle with your grandfather and choose your words carefully. They'll have to last him a long time.'

Arrianna's eyes filled with tears as the six stepped into the embracing energy of the magnificent crystal star. When the points of the star rose up once again to enfold them, they departed just as spectacularly as they'd entered. Arrianna's brush with her own destiny was over.

Apart from Wolf's gentle panting, the chamber was completely silent.

'And now we're down to two,' thought Arrianna. Grandfather placed his arm around her shoulder and guided her swiftly and silently out of the inner Star Chamber and through the antechambers into the Ancient Halls. She was physically and emotionally drained.

'I'm taking you to my chamber Arrianna. You must rest, but first we will talk a little.'

He took her into a largish chamber. It was simply furnished with clean lined energy pieces. Along the entire length of one wall were more of the ancient carvings she'd seen earlier.

'Symbols of our history' he'd explained. 'They're like signatures written in stone. Relics, if you like. Without them our people would have little knowledge of the beginning.' Arrianna was sitting on the edge of another wonderfully soft bed and Grandfather was sitting beside her. It was as it had always been. Back together for however long. She traced the fine veins on the back of his hand with her fingers and her eyes never left his face. They spoke of many things. Grandfather's other life on Earth and his departure from Earth were put aside as they reminisced about happier times. They made their peace with each other. Their conversation inevitably brought them round to Theo.

'How will I ever explain all of this to Theo? He's never going to believe me. In fact, I don't even know if I should tell him, but how can all of what's happened to him be explained so that he will understand?' She waited for Grandfather to respond. His eyes were filled with so much love and compassion, she knew he was finding these precious moments they had together unbearably sad. He reached across and held her and Arrianna knew in that instant he was going to go.

'When that time comes with Theo Arrianna, you will have to make a decision. You will know what the best thing to do for Theo will be. Kodo will help you. He can call on me and I can help Theo forget most of what happened to him. He will remember only being away from home for several days, but the rest he will have no memory of. Stay strong in the days ahead. All you have to fear is fear itself.' He broke off. The tears were streaming down Arrianna's face. Grandfather's hand was shaking as he put it inside the lining of his robes and pulled something out.

'I want you to take this with you. It will be your talisman and protect you with the power of seven. Wear it in the coming days and if you are in danger of any sort, all you need do is touch it. Help will come.' The exquisite necklace lay in the palm of his hand. Seven beautiful little aqua crystal stars. She could find no words as he placed it gently around her neck. 'I must go and join the others, Arrianna. We are running out of time.' She sensed his urgency but didn't want to accept it. Panic rose in Arrianna. She held onto him tightly and couldn't or wouldn't let go.

'Will I ever see you again?' she sobbed uncontrollably. When she stepped back she saw his tears.

'You must be brave my darling girl: In here I am with you always.' He placed a hand on his heart and the other on Arrianna's. 'My heart is your heart.' His eyes sought out hers, letting the image of the beautiful woman Arrianna had become imprint itself on his brain one last time. He rose then and walked through the chamber door.

Arrianna watched the space where Grandfather had last stood. She knew then he was finally gone and the thought of that haunted her. Wolf jumped up onto the bed and sat quietly alongside her. She buried her head in his furry mane and cried 'til she thought her heart would break all over again.

Chapter 7

It was a long time before Arrianna controlled her grief. Sleep, when it came, was disturbed and littered with fleeting cameo snapshots of Star Beings and coded symbols she was on the verge of deciphering. Wolf, sensing her distress, had tried. He moulded his long canine body along her back and rested one of his large padded paws on her hip, but she could find no real comfort from his presence. Her mind was full of haunting images of Grandfather as he'd placed the necklace around her neck and turned to leave. The sense of being forced into facing bereavement a second time by his parting was too much. She felt consumed from within. Having to experience such deep emotional chasms was exacting a heavy toll and destroying any sense of reality she had. She knew the thought was ludicrous but she thought it anyway. A large gaping hole was opening up and creating a void where her heart should have been. All the love of Astaurias could do nothing to help the physical ache inside her. If this was all part of fulfilling her destiny as Lady Samia had said, it didn't bode well for her own sanity.

Something strange had happened. Arrianna sensed at once that everything had somehow changed. She could still feel the warmth pressed up against the curve at the back of her knees, but the sensation had changed entirely. In that moment of realization she knew Wolf was gone. She opened her eyes and twisted her body away from the bed she lay on until her feet touched the ground. The first shock came with the knowledge she was back in her room on familiar home ground. It felt good. The second thing she noticed was she was now back into her own clothes. Her little antique bedside clock chimed twelve and it was light outside. Stranger still, a Jack Russell now occupied the space Wolf had vacated. She stared at its black and white markings and sturdy little body without understanding why. Arrianna had no recollections whatsoever of her return to Earth. Her mind just drew a blank. And now there was this strange dog looking at her. What was going on?

'It's alright ... it's just me ... Wolf.' The message couldn't have been clearer. She blinked and looked again. The dog was still there. Now she was more confused.

'Wolf?' she said out loud. 'Is that really you? I thought ...' Before she could finish the sentence there was a soft rap on the door. She was about to say 'Come in' but Kodo hadn't waited. He opened the door and walked into the room. His long, loose clothing had been discarded, replaced by dull, almost scruffy looking jeans and a sweatshirt. In his hand he was carrying a long wooden walking stick. It all looked slightly incongruous, seeing him dressed that way. He didn't appear to be limping so what was the stick all about? For the first time in her life Arrianna was acutely aware of Kodo the man, not Kodo Grandfather's friend. It shocked her. It was crazy to think of him as anything other than family, but strange things were happening and her emotions were shot to pieces. Her mind went off at a tangent as she flirted with senses in completely uncharted areas. He was older than her, but now she was an adult she thought rather unconvincingly to herself, the gap didn't seem too wide. In fact, she tried to rationalize to herself, there were times he looked younger than her father would have been.

Arrianna gave herself a good shaking. What sort of thoughts were they to be having about Kodo? She felt embarrassed for herself, but she couldn't forget the parting look he'd given her in Astaurias. It had meant something, but what? She could tell nothing from the way he was looking at her now. He was an unknown quantity as far as affairs of the heart were concerned. Even supposing there was someone in his life, he wouldn't tell her anyway. Why should he? Arrianna felt awkward for allowing her thoughts to be so transparent. She closed her eyes and turned her head away. When Kodo spoke to her though, there was a familiar at ease tone to his voice. He stated the obvious.

'So you're awake then?' He nodded in the direction of the bed. 'I see you've met Jack, or should I say Wolf. He's small admittedly, but still just as beautiful.' There was a wicked look in his eye as he said it. 'A true master of disguise if ever I saw one.' The humour disappeared from Kodo's face. He paused reflectively. 'It was Gaelun's idea he should come.' The mention of Grandfather's name brought the sad feelings rushing back, but Kodo allowed her no time to dwell on them. She became aware of sound coming from one of the other rooms in the house. 'We'll have to make a move soon Arrianna. The quicker we get to the portal, the quicker we get through.' He turned to face the door. 'Yula and Nikolai are raiding your food cupboards for some light provisions. You're not going to feel much like eating anyway once we enter Skerrilorn.' It wasn't the best wake up call she'd ever had, but she sensed the need for urgency and her mind turned to other practicalities. Arrianna knew by the way he was transferring his weight from one foot to the other, Kodo was anxious to get things underway.

'What about the police and neighbours?' she asked. 'Won't they think it strange if I up and leave in the middle of an investigation about Theo?' Kodo had been busy. He already had that in hand.

'I've taken care of all that. You're going away for a couple of days that's all. If they need to contact you, I've given them the phone number of friends of mine in Farsdale. I don't imagine there will be any calls, but if there are Daniel and Helen will deal with them. Now ... get a few things together. Wear some warmer clothing and remember, only carry with you what you think you're going to need. Where do you keep your car keys? I'm going to need them.' Arrianna couldn't resist.

'Why?' she asked.

'We'll need your car to take us to Alverton Abbey,' came the short response.

'God, he could be infuriating at times,' she thought. She still didn't know why they needed to travel all that distance to visit an abbey.

'Because, Arrianna,' Kodo drew it out. 'The abbey is almost two hours' drive from here and that's where Karalan's portal is.' He almost sounded irritated. 'You're going to have to work much harder on concealing your thoughts. It could prove to be dangerous in Skerrilorn if you don't.' Arrianna acknowledged it for the rebuke it was. She didn't like it much but she accepted it.

'Well ouch ... and over and out to you, too,' she muttered beneath her breath at Kodo's retreating figure. Wolf jumped off the bed and followed Kodo as he walked back out through Arrianna's door. If she never saw another person walk away from her again it wouldn't be a day too soon.

They all travelled light. Nikolai had a small rucksack on his back but that was all. She'd meant to ask Kodo about his walking stick but he'd been busy bundling everyone into the car at the time. It wasn't important. She knew that even though she was part of the team he was keeping things on a strictly need-to-know basis. Grandfather would have said it was just Kodo's protective instincts coming to the fore and Kodo was after all doing what had been asked of him. He was trying to look out for her. In her own way she was relieved and grateful. She promised herself right then she would be more understanding of the pressures he must be under to get not only her into Skerrilorn, but to get herself and Theo out. She knew she didn't have the knowledge or possess the skills the others had, but she would pull her weight just like every other member of the team.

It was odd seeing Nikolai and Yula out of their own environment. What did it feel like for them coming back to Earth like that after having spent most of the last decade or so on Astaurias? She was making that assumption about Nikolai, but she really didn't know what his story was. Arrianna had no idea if they'd been asked to come on this mission or had simply offered. She wasn't privy to that sort of information. They were dressed in warm, casual clothing just like herself. Kodo was the only one out of the four to have no outer protective wear and she was a little curious about that. She caught him looking at her in the car mirror and curbed the temptation to think about his needs at all. Lesson learned. The moment passed.

Nikolai sat silently in the front of the car and Arrianna was left to study the finer details of the back of his head. He wasn't the most sociable person she'd ever met. Kodo was driving, concentrating on the road ahead. Arrianna knew Nikolai was capable of speech. She'd heard him speaking to both Yula and Kodo several times. He always kept it to a minimum, but so far he'd barely acknowledged Arrianna's existence, let alone address her. It made her feel uncomfortable. She wondered if setting foot on Earth had resurrected memories he'd rather have forgotten. Yula was more forthcoming. She was much more relaxed around Arrianna and Arrianna liked her. Maybe if they'd met under other circumstances things might have been different. They might have had the chance to be friends. That thought pulled her up short when she remembered just why Yula was there.

The coast was left behind as they took the most direct route across country to the abbey. The countryside looked beautiful, but everyone's minds were preoccupied with what lay ahead. Small towns and pretty little villages with chocolate box cottages were passed with only the most cursory glance. The further inland they went, the fewer houses they encountered. When they left the main roads and travelled on the narrower country roads, Arrianna knew they weren't far from their destination. Wolf was getting restless sitting between herself and Yula. He kept wanting to jump up behind the seats and look out of the rear window. Kodo found it distracting. Yula and Arrianna did not.

'Get down, Wolf. I can't see a damn thing.' Wolf did as he was told, but in his own time. Arrianna pulled him over onto her knee and tried to settle him. It couldn't be too much further could it? A few miles further up the road they saw a small painted sign for Alverton Abbey. Partially obscured by dense foliage and unkempt hedging, it wasn't in the best position to be seen. The signpost pointed to another road, which was little more than a track. Arrianna had once gone on a field trip to the abbey when she'd been in primary school, but it had been so long ago she couldn't remember an awful lot about it. She knew the abbey had closed down and the Abbot and monks had moved elsewhere but that was as much as she knew. She couldn't even begin to imagine how in the space of such a relatively short time it had gone from being a self-sufficient abbey into a portal for Karalan.

Kodo slowed the car down and put the gears into second. The track was neglected and every few yards they came across another deep pothole. It wasn't meant to encourage people. A few hundred yards of this and even the most determined could easily be dissuaded from going any further. All along the track brambles and thorny bushes had laid claim to the land. Further back through the gaps the ground started to rise and where it did a tree line started. Kodo veered off the track and drove the car through the roots and the shrubs towards the tree line. Kodo seemed undeterred by the damage he was inflicting on the old car's suspension. Once he reached the tree line he carefully manoeuvred the car in amongst the trees until he was satisfied it was hidden from the track. The engine stopped and he turned round in his seat to face them all.

'Well we're here. That was the easy part. What I need you to do now is to collect as many ferns and old branches as you can, then place them over the car to conceal it a little. No use drawing attention to ourselves unless we have to. When you're finished doing that we'll walk the rest of the way. It's not far.'

Everyone piled out of the car and while Wolf sought out new ground to explore and excavate they set to work. Arrianna was relieved to finally be doing something. When they put their minds to it, it didn't take long. Before they set off on foot Kodo took them aside and spoke to them again. He looked controlled but he didn't take his eyes off the track below, not even for a second.

'This is the time for caution. You'll have to be extra vigilant. Look out for anything unusual.' The three listened in silence to his short staccato sentences. 'Everyone take care and look out for each other. Keep your eyes and ears open. Don't talk unless you have to. If you see anything at all, signal with your hand. The abbey should be deserted, but this is not a safe place to be. Stick close together and follow my lead.' He turned to Arrianna and touched the collar of her shirt. 'You should tuck that necklace inside. Try and keep it hidden away from prying eyes.'

They walked as briskly as they could, always keeping within the boundaries of the tree line. As they came over a rise the Abbey came into view. It was a large, sprawling place but even from that short distance Arrianna could sense the sadness. No sound, no people, not even a breath of wind. It was abandoned and neglected. Kodo increased the pace as they walked down onto the lower ground. They got to within twenty feet or so of the main ancient medieval door when they heard the voices. Kodo froze in his tracks.

'Watchers! Get down!' No one moved. They all crouched down and made use of the remaining covering around them. Wolf went down on all fours and crawled across the open space which separated him from Arrianna. Kodo placed a finger to his lips. They understood. A girl walked through the doorway and out into the open. She was holding the hand of a blond, curly headed boy of about ten. Neither appeared distressed or upset in any way. In fact the girl looked like any other normal teenage girl would. When the figure of a man, possibly in his early twenties, followed her out, everything suddenly changed. Arrianna immediately sensed a heavy, negative energy surrounding the three figures. She didn't like the man, not one little bit. He made her skin crawl. He wasn't tall but he was stocky. His hair was bleached blond and spiky. Dressed in a black hooded tracksuit and trainers he came and stood directly behind the girl. His voice was cold and devoid of any emotion except outright fury.

'I'm not telling you again, Niki. Just help me get him to the portal. We're going through. I don't care how we do it, just do it! He's already held things up long enough. I want this done!' He pushed hard against the girl's back and she stumbled forward, taking the boy with her. The boy tripped and fell to the ground, grazing his knee. As he picked himself up, he looked from the girl to the man. He was clearly nervous and uncertain of what was going on. No one enlightened him. The girl started to remonstrate with the unnamed man.

'I'll take him to the portal but that's all. I'm not going through it with you, no way! You promised if I got him here that would be it, job over. I am not going back with you to that hellhole. I'm never going there ever again, no matter what you say!' She was angry and defiant as she turned on the man, but he hadn't finished with her, not by a long way. He grabbed her by the hair and yanked her round until his face was only inches away from hers.

'Oh yes you are little Niki. You're definitely coming back with me. Did you honestly think all you had to do was bring him here then I'd let you go? You must be stupider than I thought. Besides,' he paused. 'The Slakers want you back. They think you have a problem with discipline. I have to say I agree with them.' From her crouching position, Arrianna still managed to see the panic on the girl's face at the mention of the Slakers. Any option or advantage the girl thought she might have had were gone and she reacted to that. She brought her booted foot down hard onto the man's and twisted away from his grip. Her voice was shrill and desperate as she called out to the boy 'Run! Get away from here. Head back for the road and don't look back.' It took a second or two for the words to sink in. The boy looked frantically around, trying to find his bearings, then turned on his heels and ran.

The girl was quick but the man was quicker. When she made a run for it he overtook her and brought her crashing to the ground. She was badly winded by the tackle. It was a total mismatch with everything stacked in the man's favour. Arrianna watched in horrified silence as the man rolled her over and head-butted the girl full in the face. Her head and neck snapped back. She had been hit with such force her head bounced off the ground then sprung back up again. In less than a minute all resistance had gone. The girl's hands flew to her face. She groaned, and then was still. Satisfied that the girl would no longer prove to be a problem, the man scanned the area then got to his feet and took off after the boy. Arrianna's temper rose along with the hackles on Wolf's back. How could someone do that to a defenceless girl like that? She swivelled her head round to look for her three companions but they had concealed themselves well.

'Do something!' her mind screamed. 'We've got to do something to help her!' but even before she could voice her next thought a stern warning came from Kodo.

'Arrianna, be quiet! We can do nothing to help her or the boy. Nothing. Now close down your thoughts or you'll blow our cover!' Arrianna wasn't satisfied with that response. Kodo and the others might be able to sit back and do nothing but she was damned if she would. She heard the movement behind her and tried to turn her head, but Kodo got to her first. With one arm tightly around her waist he pulled her hard into his own body. His other hand went over her mouth and he placed his own mouth right up against her ear. Indignation at his unwarranted action shot through her. Her first reaction was to break his hold but she only ended up being held tighter. There was real fury in Kodo's voice but he kept it low and barely above a whisper. Arrianna felt her own body stiffen in response. She prepared herself for the inevitable ticking off she knew was coming.

'You will do nothing. We will do nothing! Do you understand?' His fingers spread out and the pressure around her mouth increased. 'We can't take this on. They have to go through the portal and so must we. If we interfere now we're so close to the portal we'll be giving away any advantage we have.' The force Kodo was exerting on her was getting uncomfortable. Arrianna was not happy. She could feel his breath breathing down on her. 'I know you're angry, we all are, but for now I need you to do as I say. Can you do that?' Arrianna didn't want to agree with him, but she did. She nodded. Kodo removed his hand and placed it on her shoulder. The anger had gone from his voice. 'Good. Now we're all going to have to be still and patient for just a little longer.'

Arrianna's spirits plummeted when the man and the boy came back into view several minutes later. The boy's bid for freedom had been short lived. He was crying and unsurprisingly there was no sign of a struggle as the man frog-marched him over to the girl who was now sitting up. Her face was covered in blood and with the sleeve of her flimsy jacket she tried to wipe it away. The man stepped forward and prodded her with his foot. He was in no mood for any further discussion or aggravation.

'Get up. We're going inside. Don't go trying anything stupid like that again Niki, right?' When Niki took longer than he thought acceptable he prodded her again and repeated himself. 'Right, Niki?' The girl had nothing left.

'Right,' came the dulled response as she picked herself up off the ground. Shoulders were hunched and down for two at least. They turned in defeated, lacklustre fashion and walked slowly before disappearing through the doorway into the heart of the abbey. The voice of the man, still raised in anger, faded as he finally stopped harassing and berating his now two compliant wards.

Arrianna glanced at her watch and was surprised to see it was so late in the afternoon. The light was already beginning to fade. In the distance she could hear crows with their sharp raucous cries fly to rest high up in the bare branches of the ancient chestnut trees. She made a move to stand up but Kodo's hand stopped her.

'Wait,' he said. 'Another five minutes and they'll be gone.' To Arrianna it felt like the longest five minutes of her life. She was acutely aware of her proximity to Kodo and the effect it was having on her. It made her feel nervous. He made her feel nervous. Her heart rate picked up and her hands became clammy and sweaty. She could feel the blush creep up over her cheekbones and into her hairline. To try and conceal this, she rubbed her hands together, then rubbed her cheeks giving the impression she was just warming herself. Just how pathetic was that, she asked herself? What the hell was going on? Why was she feeling like this? All her life she'd felt happy to be around Kodo. Now she felt distracted and uncomfortable. How was it possible in just twenty-four hours to feel so differently about him? Arrianna tried to do what she had been told often enough to do. She tried controlling her thoughts but all that succeeded in doing was to confuse her further. Kodo was always so perceptive. He had to be aware of her turmoil, and she hated that.

The five minutes ended up taking ten. They were all still crouching when they heard a loud noise, swiftly followed by a bright pulsating light coming from inside the abbey. It filled it up and shone through the tall arched windows and out through the open doorway. Arrianna was reminded of the energy she'd seen in Astaurias as it swirled and moved with a life of its own. The whole building glowed from within. From nowhere a wind picked up lifting the trodden, rotting leaves underfoot. The light evaporated as quickly as it had come, then there was silence. Kodo took his hand off Arrianna's shoulder then turned to Nikolai and Yula. 'It's alright. You can come out, the coast is clear. You can relax.' He let out a sigh and did just that. They regrouped, glad to be stretching their legs, but each still very conscious of what had taken place. Arrianna still felt shaken and when she glanced at Yula she could tell she'd also been affected. Nikolai remained impassive and said nothing.

There was a definite chill in the air as the last rays of the watery autumn sun merged into the fragmented, low lying clouds and disappeared behind the tree line. Very fine drops of rain started to fall as they made their way inside the abbey. Nikolai didn't immediately join them, preferring instead to stay outside. Arrianna watched as he walked to the small graveyard with its simple wooden crosses tucked in behind some old yews and copper beech hedging. It was a beautiful final resting place for many of the monks who'd dedicated their lives to the Abbey.

It was dark inside the vestibule and darker still inside the main abbey. Apart from an inner sanctum with rows of wooden pews where the monks would have prayed, all that remained in the vast interior was a small altar table and a few discarded candles left lying in the tiny stone alcoves. Those and the graves outside were the only reminders of the monks who'd once lived there. Kodo pulled out some matches and lit a few candles. There was a faint echo as he spoke to Yula and Arrianna.

'We'll be here for a couple of hours. I suggest when Nikolai returns you take the opportunity to eat a little. Meanwhile, I'm going to stretch out.' He lay down on one of the long pews and with Wolf curled in against him they both closed their eyes.

Almost to the minute Kodo opened his eyes again. He stood up and looked at them.

'Everyone ready?' The meagre light from the candles made it impossible to see the expression on his face. Now the time had come, Arrianna began to feel apprehensive and a bit nauseous. She had no idea what to expect from the portal experience. 'Stick close together you two,' he nodded at Nikolai and Yula. 'I want one of you to hold Wolf when we go through. Arrianna, stay by my side at all times.' He must have seen the fear in her eyes. He smiled at her. 'You'll be okay. You're with friends, remember?'

Nikolai carried a single candle and Yula carried a squirming Wolf. They made their way to the back of the altar table. Directly in front lay a closed wooden door.

'Right, everyone,' Kodo shouted. He took hold of Arrianna's hand and walked straight through the door. The light blinded her and she closed her eyes. She felt like Alice toppling down the rabbit hole, only this was no ordinary hole and she was moving at phenomenal speed. Her body was sucked into an incredible, bottomless vortex of light. The force was so great all breath was expunged from her insides. She could feel Kodo's hand as he struggled to hold onto her. Just when she couldn't imagine it could get any worse, the brilliant light was extinguished and she found herself surrounded by a chilling, all consuming darkness. They were finally through the portal.

Chapter 8

Arrianna could feel the rough, uneven texture of the stone wall as it dug deep through her clothing and pressed hard against her shoulders and into her spine. When she straightened her legs and stretched them out on the filthy, open dirt floor, she was in too numbed a state to even care. Yula and Nikolai were huddled together, heads facing that same floor a few feet away from her. Wolf was trembling with tiny spasms coursing through his body and down into his legs. He looked miserable and couldn't control his shivering. His tail was still up but his harlequin ears were flat against his skull. Arrianna reached forward and dragged his unprotesting body across the floor towards her. She unzipped her jacket even wider, pulled him inside right up against her and shared the jacket's warmth. The erratic thud of his heartbeat pounded against her rib cage. It didn't lessen any when she wrapped her arms around him and supported his wiry body with her own.

'Everyone okay?' Kodo asked distractedly, but with no real conviction. He could clearly see everyone wasn't. They remained silent, staring fixedly ahead and just nodded anyway. Arrianna was drained of energy. Her trousers were ripped open at the knee and her hair felt as though it had been ripped out by the roots. She looked at the others and they didn't appear to have fared any better. They looked dishevelled and devoid of colour or any facial expression. Nikolai was gingerly fingering a fresh bruise high up on his forehead. When he caught Arrianna looking at him he stopped and turned his head away. Arrianna couldn't be bothered to try and work out again why he was the way he was with her. She'd had it with him. The next move would be up to him.

Kodo was the only one standing. Perhaps the walking stick helped to keep him upright. He showed little outward sign of having come through anything at all, but he was restless. He walked away from them, keen obviously to check on their surroundings. It gave the rest of the group the quiet time they needed to collect their thoughts and pull themselves together again. Arrianna looked around her to get a sense of her bearings. They'd come through the portal into a derelict building where only one door appeared to be intact. Most of the roof had gone and directly overhead splintered, darkened roof timbers lay at improbable angles, threatening to topple at any given moment from their precarious high positioning. Walls were barely able to support the remnants of the roof's weight. They were cracked and crumbling and full of a slimy green substance and odious oversized fungus. The surface of the floor wasn't any better. It was damp, cold, and littered with broken glass and large, unyielding stones. Someone at sometime had lit a fire with fallen shards of wood and the earth beneath was scorched and full of powdery remains and long, rusty nails. The smell in the place was dreadful but the energy in the place was a hundred times worse. What little air Arrianna tried to breathe in was heavy and laden with ominous looking particles and a sticky fine spray. She could feel it cling to every part of her. It was her turn now to shiver as she tried to brush the sensation aside. It was an impossibility. She couldn't, and it clung on regardless. Any feeling of optimism she was trying her best to nurture quickly evaporated as something very nasty began to eat away at her self-confidence. She swore she could sense herself being forced into a subtle form of controlled physical and mental submission. It frightened her. This was just the beginning of their quest and already she was discovering that this place held only darkness and confusion. How many forgotten ones had come through this particular portal and had their lives destroyed by Karalan? A little flicker of something built up inside her. Right there and then Arrianna made a commitment to herself. Here was one life he wasn't going to destroy.

There was a sudden movement from Yula as her hands flew to her mouth to stifle the scream. Arrianna followed her eyes as she sat transfixed at the sight of a rat scaling the rafters. For some reason known only to Yula, she bumped herself across the floor and moved closer to her. Arrianna was no fonder of rats than Yula, but if it helped Yula to think otherwise then that was fine with her.

Arrianna heard the dull sound of boots scraping across the floor as Kodo returned and knelt down on one knee beside them. He didn't appear anxious in any way. If he was nervous he was hiding it well. His voice was calm and even and marginally more reassuring than Arrianna had thought it would be.

'We're going to move soon. The roads are clear. If we head west we should make good headway before nightfall completely closes in.'

What constituted dark? Arrianna asked herself. As it was, they would be struggling to keep their footing in this place. Any darker and it would be almost impossible to see where they were going.

'Now remember what we've talked about. Look out for anyone, especially Slakers. If we come up against any, we'll deal with that then. If we're outnumbered by them, we pretend to be Watchers ourselves. Don't be intimidated by them. Stand up for yourselves. They'll expect that. Use all the skills of subterfuge you possess to extricate yourself from any bad situation. Try not to be side tracked or distracted if we come across any forgotten ones. Our own Star Beings will be here soon. They'll help them when the time comes. Any one of you could get separated from the group and if that happens, stay put! I'll find you. Finally …

and I know I'm repeating myself here, I'm reminding you all again about the Slakers. They still have powers like shape-shifting and telepathic transference.' He stopped to study their faces, making sure they'd taken in his words. 'Just be extra aware around them, and please ... be safe. We can't afford injuries which could hold up our mission. That would be playing right into Karalan's hands.' He stopped talking and leant forward and touched every one of them with his own healing energy. It felt like a blessing from the dear and special friend he was. 'We're going to do this!' His mouth widened into an all-inclusive smile. 'Be strong and take courage from each other.' With those words and that parting gesture he stood and prepared to leave. He'd inspired Arrianna and lifted her own confidence in herself. How long would it last?

The land outside the building surprised Arrianna. She'd expected a flat, barren wilderness but the ground was undulating. The road ahead was sided by hills which rose and fell away only to rise again. The vegetation was sparse and there were even a few scraggy trees at intervals along the road. How anything at all could survive on the nutrient deficient soil was attributed solely to the relentless determination of Mother Nature to redress the balance. She wasn't yet ready to release her powers to the destructive elements which would destroy her. Even here she was fighting for her survival. So long as hope lived on, she could do no less. The light was the worst thing. It was practically negligible. That time of day when daylight had gone but total darkness hadn't fully taken over. Arrianna couldn't begin to imagine what it must be like living in a universe where daylight never touched her face; a place where cruelty was the only thing people understood and a place where no beauty of any description existed. There could be no spark of anything except darkness in the hearts of those who were forced to stay in this bleak, depressing universal hell.

Talking was kept to a minimum as they set off in a westerly direction along the single road. Arrianna assumed it was west, but she didn't really know. Without the sun it was difficult to tell. Kodo knew and that was all that really mattered. He and Nikolai were setting a brisk pace. It was up to Yula and herself to keep up with them. Wolf was warmed and glad to be down on the ground, but it didn't take long for them all to feel the cold start seeping through their clothing again. Arrianna tucked her hair inside her jacket and pulled it close up around her neck. The pace being set kept the blood pumping but her head and bare knee were open to the damp, dank atmosphere. Living as a child in a warm climate wouldn't be helping Yula either. She was bound to be feeling it, probably more so than herself. She looked across at her and gave a good performance of a confident smile as they increased their steps to keep up with the men.

They'd been walking for a good two hours and thankfully no one had seen anything to cause them any concern. They'd even begun to relax a little. The land had changed and from what she could see, Arrianna thought they were working their way down into a narrow valley. On either side she could just make out the shapes of a low mountain range. They walked another few hundred yards, then Kodo stopped. He didn't even bother to turn round.

'Building up ahead,' he shouted over his shoulder. 'You know what you've to do. Take care.' That was all he said. Arrianna could barely see anything up ahead let alone a building, but Yula pointed to the tiny lights in the distance and she could vaguely make them out. Arrianna thought they'd go off road and bypass the building but they didn't. Kodo walked straight towards it. Before they even reached it, the sound of dogs cut across their path. The closer they got, the louder and more frenzied they became.

The building turned out to be no more than a long dilapidated shed with plenty of dimly lit windows all the way around it. Arrianna could make out movement from inside but had no idea how many people there were or whether they were Watchers or Slakers or both. She sensed the tension in the group as Kodo leant heavily on his stick and started to move forward with a definite limp. Arrianna was too busy watching the dogs. She was relieved they were chained up. They strained to break free but remained unrewarded. They never stopped barking and snarling and finally in sheer frustration they ended up turning on each other. There were yelps of submission and excited yaps of dominance gained before a side door opened to reveal the figure of a man.

'Stop your infernal yapping you bloody animals!' he bawled. Something was thrown at them, but Arrianna could only wonder as she saw the dogs cower and shy away. The figure turned and looked at the group. Nikolai's body stiffened a little. Kodo stood alongside him and they both held the man's gaze. It was a tense moment for everyone, including the figure. Arrianna and Yula knew their place in this male dominated environment. They stood behind the two men and waited. Arrianna was busy concentrating on what she should or shouldn't be doing. It wasn't until the man stood aside with a surly, distrustful look and gestured to come inside that she realized she was facing her first Slaker! His lips were drawn so tight she thought they would disappear altogether into his face. Not one word passed those lips. He watched closely as they walked past into the shed's interior. Once he was satisfied with Kodo and Nikolai his eyes latched on to Yula. He slammed the door shut and Wolf was left outside. The cuff of Arrianna's jacket accidentally brushed against his long, bony fingers and the remains of his chewed-off fingernails. The very thought of him having any contact with her made her want to vomit, until she remembered Kodo's warning. She bluffed it out and stared at him, then she switched off all her thoughts. It wasn't easy. If ever there was a personification of evil in someone's face then it was in his. He wasn't tall and he wasn't even powerful looking, but he didn't have to be. That was just a ruse. He would put the fear of God into any mortal's heart. He was dressed in dark loose clothing similar in style to Kodo's in Astaurias. He was much older looking than Kodo, with a round, deeply lined face. Running from the hairline just above his ear right down to the side of his chin was a dark, jagged scar. The rest of his skin was pale, like chalky white parchment and stretched tightly over his prominent bone structure. There were no eyelashes or eyebrows and his eyes had lost all trace of colour or identification. It looked as though someone had taken two milky opaque orbs and stuck them straight into his empty eye sockets. They looked vile, but they were still all-seeing. Arrianna turned her head away and looked at one of the other occupants of the long, narrow room. A woman stood over an open fire, studying them all with more than a little curiosity. She looked unkempt and unwashed and her clothes had seen better days. Underneath the grime and lank, straggly hair Arrianna suspected she was probably quite pretty. The woman's eyes flew at Arrianna. The hostility was palpable. They'd only just arrived and already she'd put her foot in it. Was she ever going to learn? For one awful moment she thought the woman would come right over to her, but she didn't. Kodo stepped in. He neither gave nor expected any introductions. Instead he nodded to the Slaker and pointed to the third person in the room.

'So, who's this then? Another one for Karalan?' He exuded such self-confidence and assurance the Slaker immediately began to look at him with renewed interest. The interaction between Arrianna and the woman had been missed by the Slaker, which was good news, but he was aware that a situation had arisen and Kodo had defused it. The tension in the room was gone and Kodo made good use of that fact. He relaxed his long frame into a seat and stared at the partially hidden figure in the corner of the room. Apart from the woman poking away at the fire, everyone followed suit. Arrianna was getting that nervous feeling back and she didn't know why. Kodo seemed to be in complete control. He directed his words at the Slaker and ignored everyone else.

'We're on our way to the next holding place. We'll take him off your hands, save you the trouble.' Only when the figure stepped out of the shadow and went to stand by the woman at the fire did Arrianna see him fully for the first time. It was the young man they'd seen at the abbey.

There was a cockiness and supreme arrogance in the way he tried to stare Kodo down. His voice was dismissive and full of derision.

'No need, mate. I'm not going anywhere. I've got my own group to take to the holding place. So, thanks for the offer, but no thanks.' Kodo didn't bat an eye. He stayed cool and projecting an air of total disinterest switched his attention to the woman. Nikolai took on the young man with an attitude Arrianna never knew he possessed. His shoulders went back and his chin jutted out. She saw the knuckles in his hand stand out as it went to form a fist.

'What's your problem, mate? He's only offering, that's all. No need to be so edgy … What's wrong? You got something special in the group you don't want us to see? Something special maybe you want to keep for yourself?' It was a direct challenge and the man knew it. Nikolai stood up and immediately aggression was back in the room. As if to emphasize he wouldn't be intimidated by anyone, Nikolai stepped forward and stood in front of the man.

'You want to make something out of this? Nikolai asked through clenched teeth. The man hesitated, weighing up the odds, then backed down.

'Nah … it's okay. Not worth the hassle, mate.' The man stepped back, relieved there would be no confrontation. Nikolai hadn't finished. He notched things up a gear by pushing the man hard against the shoulder. It was pay back time.

'You know what, mate,' he said with real ice in his voice. 'I don't like you much and I think you're lying. Are you lying, mate?' and he gave him another hard shove. The man looked as though he might take a swing at Nikolai, but the woman stepped away from the fire and forced herself in between the two men. She lashed out with the backs of her hands and gave them both a resounding smack around their heads. Arrianna was as stunned as the two men. Kodo and the Slaker were laughing. The woman must have been mad to come between two testosterone fuelled young men like that. Her voice was loud and abrasive and laced with fury.

'Stop trying to pick a fight with each other! You ...' she jabbed the man in the chest. 'Go and bring them out. Let him see what you've got. Show him you've nothing to hide then maybe we'll all get a bit of peace around here!' With a hand on either hip she stood her ground and continued her muttering and scowling. The man turned and walked over to a door at the back of the room. She hadn't forgotten Nikolai as she launched into another diatribe. 'And you ... you get yourself back over there and stay out of my way!' Nikolai's face flushed but he did as he was told. He slipped off his backpack and stood quietly beside Yula.

The man was bristling with anger as he wrenched the door open. He didn't want anyone muscling in on the money he'd get for taking the group to the holding place.

'Right, you lot. Get yourselves out here now!' Yula's foot moved until it was pressing up against Arrianna. She looked at her, then followed her gaze over to where Kodo and the Slaker were sitting. They had their heads partly turned towards the open door. Both were still amused at the foolhardiness of the woman, but Arrianna didn't believe for one moment they were anything other than fully aware of everything going on in the room. The Slaker turned and looked straight at Yula. His tongue snaked out and he ran it along his lips. He disgusted Yula. She looked over at the woman and did her best to ignore him.

Arrianna was trying desperately not to catch anyone's eye. She had no desire for any entanglement with the woman. She tried shrinking lower down into her chair and watched as the first child stepped into the room. Everyone's nerves were on edge. The air and space surrounding the seven disparate adults in that room almost welcomed the uncertainty and undercurrents of distrust. The silent expectation was excruciating. A young girl with bright red hair led the group out. Of the five children bound at the wrists, not one could have been older than ten. The misery and dejection rolled off them. They didn't lift their heads and continued to look down at their feet. The young girl and the curly headed boy from the abbey hobbled out next. They were bound at the wrists and the feet. It was total submission and humiliation and one of the worst things Arrianna had seen in her life. This was a trade in human flesh and it was despicable and utterly unconscionable. She felt her eyes moisten and a lump rise in her throat.

The dogs started up again and Arrianna suddenly thought of Wolf. Where was he? They were going crazy outside. As one dog stopped another would start barking and yelping. The noise just got louder and louder.

'Damn those dogs,' the Slaker said as he dragged himself out of the meagre comfort of his seat. He and the woman walked over to see what all the commotion was about.

'Expecting more visitors?' Kodo asked curiously as he joined them at the window. Nikolai made the most of the vacated fire and stood by the young man. Neither said anything. Yula stood up and moved over beside them. It was like a game of musical chairs thought Arrianna, just before the hairs rose on her neck. Everything happened at breakneck speed after that. Kodo yelled out.

'Right Eimar ... Now!' Arrianna shot out of her seat and turned to see who he was yelling at. Kodo and the woman were standing on either side of the Slaker. Both were holding long staffs with incredible crystal white lights in their hands. Arrianna was speechless. The woman was a Star Being, and for the right side at that. Before the Slaker could react to the woman's sudden transformation, both staffs were pushed with such force they entered the Slaker's heart. There was no time for him to shape-shift or try to defend himself. He'd been too slow and would pay the price. Arrianna waited for the light to pour into the Slaker, but it didn't. The reverse was happening. His dark energy and life force were being sucked out of him directly into the staffs' light. He tried screaming but could find no sound. She watched in morbid fascination as his body diminished in size. He seemed to melt like a waxwork figure. Then he was gone. Not a trace of his once evil existence remained.

Nikolai and Yula had been busy too. They'd overpowered the young man, bound his hands and feet together, than gagged and blindfolded him. Arrianna couldn't believe what had just taken place. They'd only arrived less than ten minutes ago. How had they gained the upper hand so swiftly? She hadn't even been a part of it. It made her feel slightly superfluous and surplus to requirements. In fact she wasn't even sure just why they'd brought her along in the first place.

Outside, small bright lights rose up and came down to rest on the dogs. A few still barked then they were quiet. Kodo turned away from the window.

'Wolf's been busy. Eimar, come and meet Arrianna,' he said, as if nothing at all was out of the ordinary. Eimar was smiling at her now. She embraced Arrianna.

'Welcome, my child. I wish it had been under happier circumstances.' Arrianna was studying Kodo's face over Eimar's shoulder. He looked at her and said nothing.

Eimar and Kodo disappeared into the room where the children were. They were in there for some time. Arrianna pulled a chair over to the fire and sat with Yula and Nikolai. She still felt guilt at doing nothing at all to assist them. What if they'd been injured? What if ...? Nikolai did the strangest thing. He placed his hand on top of hers and said simply,

'Don't, Arrianna.' It was the first time since meeting he'd actually spoken to her.

Kodo and Eimar came back, but there was no sign of the children. Yula raised an enquiring eyebrow.

'They'll be okay. They're resting now. Eimar will take them back to the portal and the girl will help. God willing they'll meet some of our own and no more Watchers or Slakers.' He was so matter of fact about everything.

Hadn't any of this affected him at all, Arrianna asked herself. She nodded to the young man in the corner. 'What's going to happen to him? Will he go back through?' There was a moment's hesitation before Eimar replied.

'No ... He won't go back through. The Council wouldn't allow it. He'll spend the rest of his life here along with the other Watchers. They'll never be able to get through any portals again. Their destiny is sealed.'

Arrianna was left to think about destiny and fate. Was there no way the man could be turned back to the Light?

'He's gone too far, Arrianna. There can be no going back for his heart.' She looked at Kodo when she heard the words. His voice was full of compassion for a soul he couldn't save.

Chapter 9

No concessions were made when it came to the young man's release. He remained bound and blindfolded and left to contemplate his own fate. Having been a Watcher and relied on The Dark for so long, he would soon find his options cut off at source. He had no future as a Watcher or peddlar of forgotten ones. His future lay with the only master he had ever known. He would roam the wilderness of Skerrilorn with darkness as his only companion.

It was a strangely emotional sensation finally leading the children away from the misery of the long shed. The girl with the red hair was the weakest by far, and Kodo scooped her effortlessly up into his arms. He held her close and spoke gently to her. Part of Arrianna wanted to stay with them until they reached safety, but she knew she couldn't. They were still very nervous and confused but Eimar and Kodo had put hope back in their hearts. She hoped it would sustain them enough and give them the strength they would need to get to the portal. Release came for the dogs, too. Their chains were undone and the freedom they'd yearned was granted. Thanks to Wolf's intervention and healing, once the last chain came off everyone noticed the transformation. The aggression was gone. Many animals rolled on the ground then shook their horribly matted coats. Others were just happy to walk unhindered. Wolf was in a playful mood and he joined them for a while. Immediately their sense of freedom was established in their minds, it didn't take the dogs long to turn away and disappear into the ever darkening gloom of the night.

Arrianna was glad to be reunited with Wolf. The group was complete again. They walked Eimar and the children back out of the valley then turned to say their farewells. The young girl Niki was carrying the curly headed boy on her back. She looked shyly at Kodo.

'Thank you, mister.' Kodo's eyes were kind as he turned his group around and with Wolf leading the way they headed off in a different direction.

For hours they walked north over rough, inhospitable terrain. It was an exhausting and exacting hike into a no-man's land which was totally unforgiving. Eventually they reached an escarpment at the base of the small mountain range. They stopped and drank greedily from a bottle of water. It was clean and sweet tasting and revived their flagging spirits. Nikolai was edgy and keen to be on the move again. Arrianna kept losing her footing as the real night darkness they'd been dreading began to close in around them. Kodo didn't stop. He kept pushing them.

'Not much further,' he would shout to them. In Kodo's language that could mean two miles or twenty miles depending on how much energy he had left. Arrianna wished he would stop. They were all struggling. The path began to rise and they were now walking in single file. Yula reached back and grabbed hold of Arrianna's hand. She was shaking. Arrianna had a flashback to her childhood in East Africa. She remembered seeing elephants manoeuvre themselves into a narrow gorge to gain access to the rocks' underground minerals. The space was tight at the rock face opening, but the elephants had been going there for generations. They took their time and in single file squeezed their bodies into the confined, darkened interior. The babies had reached out blindly with their trunks and latched onto the tail in front. Arrianna knew how they felt. It was like the blind leading the blind only here it was up an escarpment. Thoughts of Africa inevitably led to thoughts of her parents and Theo. They should have been happy memories but that was an impossibility. They ended up being sad thoughts. God, how she wished she could wave a magic wand and have those good times back again.

Kodo kept climbing and climbing. It was becoming dangerous underfoot. Finally, he stopped. Arrianna doubted if any of them could have carried on much further. A giddy almost euphoric feeling swept through her body as aching limbs succumbed to gentle relief. Some way back, just off the track, something caught Kodo's attention. He walked a few more yards and called over to them.

'It's alright, I've found it. It's up here. This is where we'll spend the night.' They should have been happy, but they weren't. The prospect of a night spent on the open mountain was met with a collective groan. Then they saw what Kodo had so obviously known: a mountain hut. Not a large one, but protection from the elements just the same. Kodo covered the distance between himself and the steps of the hut in seconds. They heard Wolf yelp as Kodo stumbled over him and came down with a clatter. He cursed himself and Wolf. The final few yards brought them level with Kodo and Wolf. Everyone watched as Kodo absent-mindedly leant forward to rub the offending earth off his shin. It was the release mechanism they needed. Yula and Arrianna began to laugh.

Once inside, Nikolai opened his backpack and pulled out a couple of candles. The room wasn't exactly glowing, but there was enough light for them now to see. It was very basic. No energy beds or coverings here. In one corner lay two pallets and against one wall a small open grate for a fire. Arrianna made herself useful and placed some of the sticks and logs left beside the fire into a pile in the centre of the grate. They were damp. She went to strike Nikolai's matches, but Kodo stopped her.

'Keep the fire small. Those logs will have to last us all night.' He was tetchy and grumpy and like everyone else he was weary.

'Yes, well, chance would be a fine thing,' she muttered to herself as she struggled to get the fire going. 'I've got to get the blasted things to light first!'

Amazingly, they had hot food that night. Along with the provisions Nikolai had packed, a flat fold-away pan which Grandfather had used on their occasional camping trips was magically produced. While Nikolai opened packets and some small tins, Arrianna stirred and mixed in the contents. It was a small bonding process between the two. Nikolai's aloofness with her was forgotten and she was rewarded with a smile. Conversation within the hut amounted to nothing. The one consolation was the meal. Food had never tasted so good as they all ate from the same pan. Just as soon as they'd eaten, Arrianna and Yula lay down and shared a pallet. Nikolai stretched out on the other while Kodo sat with Wolf beside the fire and studied the map Eimar had given him. Arrianna felt the warmth of Yula's body up against her back. Within minutes they were both asleep.

Kodo's idea of a night bore no relevance to anyone else's. Just as soon as the first splinters of what passed as light filtered through the darkness, they packed up and set off on foot once more.

'We're heading here,' Kodo pointed to a spot on the crumpled, unfolded map. 'That's where Karalan's holed up with Theo.' It looked a long way off and it would be another gruelling climb, but if they hoped to conceal themselves they had to use that route. The prospect of such a climb was daunting, especially when they all knew there was a more direct route, but they had to do it. All Arrianna had to do was remember she had the freedom to climb. Theo didn't. The men were definitely anxious and that rubbed off on Arrianna and Yula. Kodo was so preoccupied with his responsibilities he hadn't said more than a dozen words since the previous night. It had a dramatic effect on everyone's spirits. Everything seemed to be resting on his shoulders. So much was expected of him but Arrianna suspected that was just a fraction of what he expected of himself. The time was fast approaching when they'd all have to confront their fears. Kodo's task was the most onerous one of all. Watchers and Slakers were bad enough, but the greatest fear was the unknown. Karalan. Arrianna remembered Grandfather's words on fear. She tried to let go of it, at least for the time being.

They walked all morning without stopping. Every muscle in their bodies ached with fatigue. They'd encountered one obstacle after another on the mountain. None of them were expert climbers and it said a great deal about the endurance of the group that they'd come so far without any major mishaps. Their luck had held and fortune was favouring them. They'd seen and heard nothing. No Watchers, no Slakers.

The end of the escarpment came when they were least expecting it. Suddenly the track came to an end. They all looked over the edge and down. A couple of hundred feet below, in between two peaks, the land flattened out into a plateau which was covered in trees. After the paucity in natural resources, it was a bizarre sight to have come across. Kodo took out his map and laid it on the track.

'That is Skerrilorn's only surviving forest. It stretches from here, right up to there.' Kodo followed the map with his finger. 'It's going to take hours to get to, but this,' he stabbed the map with his forefinger, 'this is where we'll find Karalan. I'm warning you now, there's a holding place in the centre of the forest. We'll have to go around it to get to Karalan.'

The map was folded away as everyone realized that for the first time they were within striking distance of Karalan. Of course that also meant he was within striking distance of them. It was a salutary lesson in getting ahead of themselves. They still had the forest to negotiate. No one thought for a moment that would be like a stroll in the park.

They bumped and slid their way down the steep stony incline until their eyes were level with the trees. Arrianna thought if one part of her backside was without a bruise she'd be amazed. They helped each other up and walked out across the open ground towards their camouflage and a feeling, for however long, of safety.

Arrianna heard a noise high overhead. She strained to look and was surprised to see a large flock of birds. They were the first she'd seen since they came through the portal. Everyone turned and looked up. Kodo's reactions were like lightning. He shouted at the top of his voice.

'Razors ... Start running!' Arrianna was slow to grasp the immediacy of the situation, but when everyone started running full pelt towards the trees she didn't hesitate and ran as fast as the surface would allow her to. It wasn't fast enough. Her neck jarred forward as something hit her from behind and clawed at her head. It was one of the birds. More followed. They dive bombed her and came at her from all angles. It was impossible to protect herself and run at the same time. She watched as one bird turned with precision timing mid air and flew straight towards her. The dull opaqueness of its eyes passed by in a blur of motion as it swooped down and clipped the side of her face. She cried out and raised her hands to protect herself. That only incited them further. Yula and Nikolai were ducking and shouting, trying to ward off the attack, but as soon as one bird drew blood, another took its place. It wasn't just the faces they went after. Any unprotected part of the body was attacked. The birds were relentless and would not give up. Arrianna's face and hands were stinging. Her scalp felt as though it had been raked by something long and sharp. It hurt. They still hadn't reached the trees, but fit as she was, her legs wouldn't pump any faster. It was becoming impossible to out run the birds. Her mind registered the slight dip in the ground but it was too late to alter her stride. She tripped over and fell forward, landing on her knees. Pain was pushed to the back of her mind as she forced herself back on to her feet again. Just when she thought she wasn't going to make it, the birds were hit from all sides with the full force and power of Kodo's staff. The area above the group lit up with the brilliance of its rays. Not one bird was left flying as the entire flock fell out of the sky and landed on the open ground around them. Many of the bodies were mangled and ripped apart. Others remained oddly complete. They were all dead. Everyone stopped running to look down at their aerial attackers. Seeing them like that made them appear like any normal flock of birds, but they all knew there was nothing at all normal about them. They were black all over, about the size of regular starlings. That was all they had in common with their Earthly, feathered brothers. Their beaks were broader and finely pointed, their feet clawed and horribly barbed. The greatest damage had been done with their wing feathers, which were long and razor sharp and bore the markings of their victims' blood. It was a scene of utter carnage which revolted them all.

Kodo was keen to create distance between himself and the lifeless forms. He reached the edge of the tree line while the rest of the group remained standing in a state of shock. He opened his mouth and yelled out to them.

'Don't just stand there! Move! Get over here before anything else sees us!' They were spurred into action by the harsh tone of his voice, but no one ran on command. Instead they followed his lead until they were free of the open ground. Nothing was said as they walked dejectedly in amongst the trees. They slid down to the ground and stared at each other's dazed expressions. What the hell had just happened?

Kodo had some cuts on his bare arms but that appeared to be all. The others hadn't been quite so lucky. They were scratched and bleeding from nasty open wounds. Yula was the worst. She had a tear on her face, which had narrowly missed her eye and it was already beginning to swell up. This was not something any of them needed right now. Kodo's healing was needed, however, he wasn't volunteering his services. He stood motionless and stony faced. He allowed the silence to build up and hang over the group. Arrianna had never seen his so angry. His grip on his walking stick tightened as he smashed it hard against the side of a fallen tree. Pulse points at his temples rose under his skin as he faced them all.

'God damn it and blast it to hell!' he roared. 'Our cover's blown. You know that, don't you? Well ... Don't you?' There was a deathly hush before he continued the verbal onslaught. 'You'd all better hope help is on the way because we're finished without it.' Kodo in a rage was not a pretty sight. He was so tall and foreboding, he would terrify anyone. Arrianna was indignant at being on the receiving end of his temper, particularly since it was so unjustified. He wasn't even badly hurt compared to the others, she thought rather sourly. What did he have to complain about? Why was he being such a pig?

'No,' she corrected herself quickly, 'pigs were nice creatures. He was being a boor!' No one was happy, but it wasn't the group's fault the Razors had attacked. The birds had come out of the blue, entirely unprovoked. No one could have expected them to attack like that. Now Kodo was attacking them, too. Arrianna wasn't very level headed when it came to her own temper. She could erupt in seconds and that's exactly what she did. She turned to challenge Kodo.

'Now just hang on a minute, here. You're not seriously saying we're to blame for what's just happened, are you?' She took the same stance as Kodo had. 'Well ... are you?' she demanded. Arrianna's voice could drip ice with the best of them. She wasn't about to spare Kodo from some verbal haranguing of her own. Her eyes focused right in and onto him. He wouldn't look at her. This enraged her more. How could he think they were to blame? It was just so stupid. They wanted their mission to succeed just as he did. They'd climbed over bloody mountains for him, for God's sake! When it got right down to it, why hadn't he seen this coming? Where were his miraculous powers of perception when they really needed them? Everyone heard the verbal and mental exchange. Yula and Nikolai decided sensibly to stay out if it. Kodo didn't answer Arrianna. He deliberately ignored her and turned to Yula instead. No attempt was made at civility. Arrianna wanted to hit him.

'Yula! Wolf! You two come with me. We'll see what's up ahead. None of us wants any more surprises, do we?' He spoke to Nikolai with the same curt tone. Nikolai held his gaze and refused to be intimidated by his ill-natured attitude. 'Take care of her. See if you can't calm her down a little.' Kodo nodded in Arrianna's direction. He turned on his heel and started to walk away. Arrianna might have been angry before. Now she was plain livid. Take care of her! Her! She leapt to her feet, determined Kodo would not have the last word on this one.

'That's right. Turn around and walk away. You're good at that! This ... is ... not ... our fault and you know it!' She used her considerable voice and not her mind this time to scream after him. As she'd expected he didn't respond.

She couldn't remember what Nikolai said to her. She was still seething. After a while his words calmed her frayed nerves and got through to her. Eventually she felt the anger drain away. She was even able to laugh at herself for being so touchy and over reacting. Kodo had provoked her. He'd known just which buttons to press, but she shouldn't have risen to the bait. Nikolai cleaned Arrianna's wounds with a little of their precious bottled water, then gave her some healing. He saw to his own wounds only after he'd taken care of her. Arrianna helped him with the deep gashes on the back of his head. A temporary peace was restored in both their minds. They sat quietly and waited for the others to return.

The group had been gone a long time, and although he didn't say it, Arrianna suspected Nikolai was starting to feel anxious again. When they heard feet trudging through the undergrowth behind them, they both breathed a sigh of relief. Arrianna turned around to welcome everyone back.

The smile froze on her face. Instead of the familiar trio, two strangers were walking towards them. Her head whipped round as Nikolai started to rise from the ground.

'Watchers,' he said quickly in a hushed tone. That was not all. Coming in off the open ground were three more. All five of them were men. Dressed in the statutory black favoured by the Watchers, there was another striking similarity. They were all young men like Nikolai and physically they looked in good shape. Three of them carried baseball bats. They had the confidence that any pack of animals used to getting their own way would have. It was terrifying. As she rose to stand by Nikolai's side, Arrianna felt the necklace beneath her shirt brush gently against her skin, a silent reminder of Grandfather and the Star Council. If every their help was needed, now would be the time. Arrianna still couldn't believe they'd been caught out so quickly after the bird attack, so how had it happened? When and why had everything suddenly gone so horribly wrong and so off course? She already knew the grim answer. When the group had split and Kodo had gone off, that had been the first mistake. The second had been in letting them go. Now they wouldn't be coming back. She knew something dreadful must have happened. There had been no great ruckus associated with a fight of any kind, and no signs of any white lights coming through the forest. They would all have returned long before now if things had been okay. She and Nikolai were completely on their own at the mercy of five unpredictable Watchers. Bile rose in the back of her throat as she struggled to remember all Kodo had taught her. She'd have to put it into practice and play the role of her life. Standing beside Nikolai gave her some confidence but what use would it be? What were they to do? What would Nikolai realistically be able to do to get them both out of this? He couldn't very well shape-shift and give Arrianna up to the Watchers. Nor did he have any magical staff of light. They could both only use what they had immediately to hand and that amounted to nothing other than their courage. They were hopelessly outnumbered and as a result they were going to play the game of survival. Their only option was to try and bluff the Watchers into thinking they were Watchers too. Arrianna didn't fancy their chances. They'd have a lot of explaining to do. Well ... here goes nothing she said just before she stared defiantly at the Watchers who had now formed a circle around Nikolai and herself. The five had the opposition exactly where they wanted them. They could take as much or as little time as they needed to get the answers they needed. Nikolai was his same cool self as he supported Arrianna's arrogant, questioning stance.

'So,' said the tallest of the Watchers nearest to Nikolai. 'What's with the dead Razors?' he asked softly but menacingly. 'What do you two know about that then?' It was a challenge, and when Nikolai looked back and the Watcher could clearly see the puzzled look on Nikolai's face, she thought the Watcher might decide to change his questioning. 'The birds lying out there ... How did that happen? And what about the light? You must have seen that. Everyone within miles saw that, so you two must have seen it too, right? Tell me about it. We really want to know, don't we fellas?' Nikolai looked around the faces but he showed no fear. He didn't flinch in his response and continued with his confident, untroubled posture.

'Yeah, we saw the light all right, but when we went out and saw all them dead animals on the ground, we'd no idea what 'ad 'appened to them. There weren't no one there. Nuthin. We looked round, course we did, but there weren't no traces of anythin'. We came in here thinkin' there might be somethin' lurkin' around here, but honest, we ain't seen one damn thing.' It was a good performance and Arrianna was impressed. The Watchers weren't. They weren't convinced about a story from a stranger they'd found roaming about in their neck of the woods. Nikolai and Arrianna's fresh injuries sealed their fate for them. The Watchers weren't stupid. The atmosphere was suffocating and the tension extreme. The Watcher who stepped right up to Arrianna was the shortest, and reminded her of a very ugly skinhead. He had bad breath and his body smelt rancid. He put his hand out to touch Arrianna's hair. The leer on his face made her want to do something physically painful to his private parts.

'Tell me, pretty lady, what have you got to say to us? What can you tell us that your partner won't?' Arrianna's mouth tightened as she lashed out and pushed his hands away from her.

'Get your stinking hands off me, you jerk! We're telling you the truth! Don't touch me again, right?' She thought she'd got away with it, but the man smacked her face with the back of his hand. Her head shot back and the top button of her shirt came undone. The Watcher's eyes immediately noticed the tips of the necklace. He reached towards her again.

'It's all right sweet lips,' he said, looking her up and down with a lascivious smirk on his face. 'I believe you, but first of all tell me, what's this?' In one swift movement he reached up towards her and ripped the necklace from her throat. The Watcher held it up for everyone to see. He swiftly switched it to his other hand as another Watcher made a grab for it.

'You ain't havin' this. It's mine. Back off, or else!' Maybe it was the 'or else' which made the other Watcher think twice. Arrianna didn't really care. She didn't stop to think. She went straight for the Watcher and tried to snatch it back, but he was too quick for her, and besides, he was enjoying seeing her so rattled.

'Give me that back!' she screamed in his face. 'You're not keeping that – it's mine!' The Watcher stomped his foot on the ground and mimicked Arrianna.

'Oh ... give me that back, it's mine!' His face was inches from hers. The expression on it changed in an instant. 'I don't think so, sweetheart,' he said maliciously, and dangled the necklace right in front of her face. 'You ain't never getting this back!' The Watchers laughed as Arrianna launched a full physical attack on their hapless friend. Nikolai made a move but the three Watchers at his back grabbed him and stopped him. They forced his arms backwards over one of their baseball bats and held another one just beside his kneecaps. He struggled to break free of their hold and go to help Arrianna. They grabbed hold of his hair and yanked his head so far back he though his neck would snap. Arrianna was in a blind, furious world of her own. Everything was clouded in a mist of her mindless desire for retaliation. She'd somehow got on to her Watcher's back and was pummelling his head with one fist and still trying to reach the necklace with the other. She had her long legs wrapped firmly around the man's middle. There was a moment when everything suddenly stilled in Arrianna's mind. The fog of fury cleared and clarity returned. Some imperceptible something had changed. She felt her eyes being drawn, and she turned and looked sideways. She saw the bird come in low, its claws fully extended, its hooked beak open and ready to strike. The tips of the feathers brushed against the side of her face. The necklace was released in an instant as the claws and beak raked across the back of the Watcher's hand. Arrianna jumped down to the ground. A barrage of expletives followed as the Watcher looked at the damage done to his hand. The bird rose high above them and landed on a branch. Arrianna's heart sang. Hawk was here! The bird's appearance threw everything into disarray for the Watchers. The two closest to Arrianna were stunned into silence. Arrianna's eyes sought out Nikolai. Then she saw something she thought she'd lost. Directly behind the Watchers holding Nikolai, Kodo, Yula and Wolf came thundering through the gaps in the trees to take on his assailants. Somehow they'd managed to double back without being seen. Wolf was back to his full resplendent glory leading the attack. As soon as the first man was struck by a blow from Kodo, the stranglehold on Nikolai was broken. He leapt sideways just as the second baseball-wielding Watcher lashed out. He missed Nikolai by inches, but managed to catch the third Watcher right across the knee. The Watcher screamed in agony and rolled onto the ground, clutching his shattered knee. Kodo yelled out over the general chaos.

'Nikolai! Catch!' A long black stick flew through the air and Nikolai twisted around and caught it with one hand. He and Kodo took care of the three Watchers whilst Yula and Wolf covered the ground and came to Arrianna's assistance. Arrianna's Watchers weren't going to be put off by a woman and a big white dog. Not at first they weren't anyway. They stood their ground and even advanced a little, but Arrianna knew in her heart that the tide had turned. She watched in amazement as Yula dropped swiftly into a full attacking mode. She held a long wooden stick with both hands and brought it down with a crack onto one of the Watcher's shoulders. She was using martial arts skills just as Kodo and Nikolai were, and the outcome after that was never in any doubt. The Watcher with the ripped hand made a break for it, but Wolf took off after him and after a struggle he brought him down. Wolf stayed with his dripping jaws over the Watcher until Kodo came over and dragged the man away.

All the group's strength was needed as they bound the Watchers with a fine nylon rope from Nikolai's bottomless backpack. The more the Watchers struggled, the tighter the rope became and the deeper it cut into their flesh. They tied them around the base of a tall sturdy tree. Kodo checked them over then touched every one of them on the side of the neck with his stick. Their heads rolled to the side and their eyes closed. They were out cold. Their Watchers were beaten and wouldn't be bothering anyone for some time. By then hopefully everything would be over.

Chapter 10

Wolf was on the freshly fallen bark and pungent smelling sprays of crushed pine needles rolling on his back. His body moved back and forth, from side to side, in a moment of instant animal gratification. When he'd finished with that, he rose and strode majestically over to lie in between Arrianna and Yula. His neck arched back and his jaws opened in a teeth-baring yawn before his head finally found a home across Arrianna's legs. Hawk sat on the same rotting tree trunk Kodo had smashed, flexing his wings and preening his glorious white flight feathers. Like a stray piece of tumbling fluffy thistledown, one floated silently to the ground and rested there, reminding the forest that Light lived on even in the darkest places. There was enormous relief all round when the Watchers were finally taken out of the picture. Everyone's body ached with the exertion. They inspected each other's wounds and cuts and dealt with the minor stuff themselves. Time was the overriding factor in everything they did and there wasn't much of that before they'd have to move on. Kodo worked swiftly and with great dexterity and skill on the more badly damaged parts of their bodies, while Nikolai and Yula worked on him. Now the initial rush of adrenalin had been expended and their bodies' sugars burnt up, they were left with little energy. They were quite simply wiped out. Kodo's warm, healing energy re-energised them and cleared their minds of unnecessary, non-essential thought. He realigned their focus on what they had to do. They had a clear perspective again.

Kodo had even found some time in between all of this to repair the damage to the necklace. The earlier slanging match between himself and Arrianna was forgotten when he placed the seven stars back around her neck with a rare tenderness. They both accepted, without anything being said, of sharing at times a capricious, volatile temperament.

'There,' said Kodo as he bent down and moved the hair away from the nape of her neck. 'Back where it belongs.' The caring, gentle side of him which he'd shown in the past was back. His hand pressed against her skin and the sensation ran straight through her. Kodo felt it too and she sensed the tremor in his hand. He fumbled with the clasp until it clicked back into place. Arrianna lifted her hand to touch the necklace and felt her fingers brush against the back of his arm. She made no attempt to remove her hand and left it exactly where it was. He was so close she could feel his breath against her face. Everything around her faded and slowly fell away. Kodo was the only thing she was conscious of. When he stepped back she saw his face. For a fraction of a second his guard dropped. She looked into his eyes and he allowed her to see the same look they'd shared in Astaurias. It was as quick as that. When he turned away he wasn't dismissive, he was in control again. Arrianna didn't feel foolish this time for having the thoughts she did. She didn't suppress them but let her heart embrace them.

The respite was short lived. Hawk had brought news of the Star Beings. They were safely through the portals and now within a few short miles of the holding places. Skerrilorn had so far been successfully infiltrated but it was a monumental undertaking and a great deal could still go wrong. The good news for the group was that their Star Beings had come through their portal just shortly after Hawk. They wouldn't be far away.

They set off and headed inwards, towards the centre of the forest. Kodo made no attempt to conceal his staff. He walked ahead with it firmly in his hands. The deeper they went in amongst the trees, the darker and more oppressive it became. Arrianna kept hearing strange slow, rhythmic sounds but had little idea where they were coming from. No one seemed unduly concerned but she remained cautious and kept her eyes peeled for anything unusual. Hawk was flying through the gaps in the trees and not above them. When he stopped suddenly mid air, everyone stopped. Nikolai and Kodo stood at the head of the group while Wolf brought up the rear. Everyone was alert now. Arrianna saw two large moth hawks fly out of a small clearing only feet away and come to hover in front of the group. There was a large flash of white light. The moths disappeared and two Star Beings stood in their place. So that was shape-shifting, Arrianna said to herself. It was amazing and so were the two Star Beings. The time for disguise was over and there could be no mistaking what they were. They were dressed in loose fitting garments of the Light and each carried a staff just like Kodo. Arrianna felt dwarfed beside them. Everyone was dwarfed, including Kodo. They were exceptionally tall and phenomenally powerful looking, and, Arrianna mused, not something you'd like to come across on a dark night. Both placed a hand on their hearts and greeted the group in true Star Being fashion.

'Finn. Zorkan.' Kodo acknowledged their greeting with one of his own. He wasted no time.

'What's the news on Karalan? Has his network of spies picked up on anything yet? Does he know we're in Skerrilorn?' Zorkan, the one with the long black hair and dark hazel eyes, shook his head.

'No. No one knows we're here, but they will. We've already destroyed several Slakers and Watchers on our way to meet you. They're going to be missed. Word is carrying on the air that all is not right. If it hasn't reached the holding places yet, it very soon will.' Kodo listened to the news but he wanted to hear more.

'What about Karalan?' he asked impatiently, but not offensively. He turned to the other Star Being. Finn had worry written all over his face but he told Kodo what they'd learnt.

'Karalan has moved. Our information was out on that one. He doesn't have Theo yet. He's on his way to the holding place to pick him up himself. Karalan never leaves his stronghold, but he's making an exception for Theo. Seems he doesn't want anything happening to Gaelun's grandson. Not yet, anyway.' Finn realized how that must have sounded, but things were the way they were. There was no use pretending otherwise. 'Maybe that will help us. I don't know. Karalan will be surrounded by his own henchmen and there are at least fifty or so Watchers and Slakers already at the holding place. We can't avoid it. We're going to have to go inside to find Theo.' Finn looked at Kodo and shook his head.

'I don't know if we'll be able to do this. How will we find Theo in amongst the hundreds of forgotten ones? How do we get him out now? Our in-and-out tactics of isolating Karalan aren't going to be much use to us without the element of surprise. As soon as we enter the holding place Karalan will have so much more protection than we'd ever thought he would.' Finn looked from Kodo to the group. His mouth was down at the corners and he couldn't quite hold their gaze. When Arrianna heard his words she really was sick. She stepped aside from the group and let the contents of her stomach hit the forest floor. Yula bent down and put an arm round her shoulder.

'Try not to think of the holding place. Kodo will find a way to get Theo out. He's good at that. He rescued me. He'll rescue Theo. We've come this far, and he won't give in that easily. Besides,' she said in a lighter tone, 'Gaelun told me Theo is a handsome young man, and I'd like him when I met him. I'm going to meet him, Arrianna. The game's not over yet.' The more Arrianna learnt of Yula, the more she admired her. She was a strong young woman who'd been through a lot. She was prepared to put her own life on the line for someone she'd only heard of a short while ago. Arrianna stood up and turned to face Yula.

'Thank you,' she said softly.

No one apart from Kodo and the two Star Beings had a realistic concept of just what it was going to take for everything now to work. What they needed was some luck and definitive news on Karalan and Theo. That and a healthy injection of self-belief that they could pull this off and still walk out of Skerrilorn with their lives intact. The original plan for the Star Beings rescuing the children could not be put on hold for the sake of one person being found. It would be up to Kodo to be in place and strike as fast as he could, if and when the information finally got through. Regardless of what was going on around him, he'd have to wait for word of Theo. There would only be one short opportunity to get him out and take care of Karalan. Life for the group had suddenly become a lot more complicated than any of them could have envisaged.

Urgency soon overrode the desire for concealment as the group took the fastest and most direct route to the holding place. Arrianna began to understand the agonies of cross-country running as she struggled to keep apace with the three front-runners. Kodo, Finn and Zorkan wove in and out of the trees with such grace and ease they left the others looking like clumsy, heavy-footed amateurs. Finally, after several miles, they slowed back down to a walking pace.

Arrianna could hear the faint rhythmic sound she'd heard earlier. It was tantalizingly close, but she still couldn't be certain what it was. Then suddenly she realized. It was the sound of sturdy gossamer wings beating furiously against the stilled air. Everyone's spirits soared when they saw the large swarm of flying insects skim over their heads and move in behind them. The cavalry had arrived! They mightn't seem particularly dangerous right now, but when the time came they'd be a formidable force to match any. Immediately they began to fan out in all directions and sweep through the forest flushing out any stray Watchers or anything from The Dark which could raise the alarm.

The group finally stopped when the trees began to thin out. Darkness was replaced with small parcels of light and up ahead in a flattened, dipped area was a massive clearing. The holding place was directly in front of them. They stayed back well within the tree line and only ventured forward to study the place more closely when they were sure it was all right to do so. Every one of them was conscious of danger arising out of nothing and they remained in a state of high alert. Arrianna was horrified by what she saw. To call it a holding place was a complete misnomer. With its barbed wire perimeter fencing and lookout towers, it was more reminiscent of a prisoner-of-war camp. It was a vast complex spread out over a large open area. They counted twenty long wooden structures in random formation within the confines of the compound. At the centre, protected on all sides by the structures, was a circular stone building built around a central domed area. Everything was laid out to look like a giant eye and it gave Arrianna the absolute creeps. The most barbaric thing was the sight of the children. There were scores of them ranging from very young to young teenagers, and that was just the ones they could see from their position. There would be just as many unseen ones. Those closest to the fencing all shared the same dazed, vacant expression. Many sat silently in groups on the bare ground, staring blankly ahead into the hollow eyes of those around them. All of them were malnourished and dirty and stripped of any ounce of hope they'd once possessed. The young ones were the most pitiful. They could do nothing to help themselves. The Watchers in the towers and around the perimeter fencing were wasting their time. These children barely had the strength to survive, let alone escape.

The anger amongst the group was tangible. A movement near one of the huts drew everyone's attention. They closed ranks and watched as a large group of Slakers, most of them armed, emerged from one of the wooden buildings and ran towards the domed building at the centre. Word of Skerrilorn's invasion was a secret no more. There would be no pre-emptive strike by forces of The Light. The word was obviously out. Arrianna could sense the subtle shift in the group. There was no alternative. They would have to move now, regardless.

Raven chose that precise moment to make an appearance. She skirted along the outer edges of the tree line and swept in to land on a low hanging branch next to Hawk. She flapped her wings to steady herself then looked down on the group and spoke to Kodo. It was the news they'd all been waiting for. Karalan was already in the camp and Theo was being held in the main part of the building the Slakers were heading towards. The ripple effect was immediate. Word spread to every Star Being now waiting in position around the camp's perimeter. The air of urgency touched everyone. Kodo moved swiftly to Arrianna's side and opened her hand. He placed a long flat knife, encased in a simple lightweight sheath across her palm, then closed her fingers back around it. His expression was grim and his speech hurried and snatched.

'This is mine, Arrianna ... I want you to take it just in case. It'll give you that little bit extra protection if you need it. Tuck it inside your belt. Keep it safe. Keep yourself safe. Now ... go with Nikolai and Yula. The Star Beings will look out for you as much as they can.' Arrianna wanted to reach out to him but there was no time. Before she could even say one single word he had turned and with Zorkan, Finn and Wolf he ran off through the trees to meet the remaining Star Beings for their attack on Karalan.

Arrianna didn't have time to think, besides, the time for words was over. The forgotten ones were their sole mission now. She slipped the knife beneath her jacket and into the space between her waistband and her belt. It fitted snugly without being a hindrance. Arrianna felt a draught as Hawk and Raven brushed over the back of the trio's heads and flew out into the open. It was the signal everyone and everything had been waiting for. The air came alive with the sounds of insects flying overhead. There were bees buzzing, hornets droning, moths flapping and ants zipping. There were butterflies bringing the first beauty Skerrilorn had known and finally there were the delicate fireflies with their beetled wings. Every one of them glowed with a crystal from Astaurias. They swept out of the forest and over the razor sharp fencing down towards the children. It was a spectacular sight to watch as lights darted around the camp, but it was ruined by the uncertainty of the outcome. The Watchers in the towers were the first to feel the real impact of the attack. The hornets swarmed over them and stung them in as many places as they could. The stings were like a double-edged sword. The Watchers would feel the stings, but, they were tipped with a strong sleeping potion as well. One determined Watcher managed to raise a general alarm before falling onto the floor of the tower in a screaming, writhing heap. A sound like a klaxon poured out across the camp until several hornets shape-shifted and closed the thing down again. Slakers began to scramble out of the wooden structures at the sound of the alarm. For every Slaker who appeared, several Star Beings would shape-shift to combat them. Insects were touching children with The Light then shape-shifting back into Star Beings at an incredible rate. The children were mesmerized and terrified at the same time as they moved swiftly from one group of children to the next. Nikolai, Yula and Arrianna reached the gates of the camp just as they swung open. They had unhindered access into the camp. There were no

Watchers to stop them as they sprinted across the open ground to the first group of children.

The whole camp was in a state of total chaos and panic. Children were screaming and trying to run away from the aerial bombardment, but there was no place for them to run to. They collided with each other and fell on top of each other. Some were struck with blows from arms as they tried to ward off the insects. Dozens of children did have The Light put back into them, and, as the others saw there was nothing to be feared, they huddled together in groups until they too could be touched. There was a beautiful moment when a Peacock butterfly landed on a thin, raggedy little girl. Her eyes lit up and she reached out tentatively to touch the butterfly's glowing body and stroke its velvety wings. For her at least the fear had gone.

The noise around them was deafening as fighting continued unabated. It was terrifying, especially for the children. Star Beings were appearing where insects once hovered to take on the Watchers still left standing. To complicate things further, the Slakers were doing some shape-shifting of their own. They weren't about to make themselves easy targets. Nikolai had done what he'd meant to do. He'd got Arrianna and Yula into the camp and to the safety of the Star Beings and the children. His talents were needed elsewhere. He went off to help in the fight. Amidst all the confusion it was inevitable that fear would take precedence over acceptance. Children everywhere were sobbing and clinging on to each other, seeking the reassurance no other child could give them. It was a vicious circle. Star Beings were moving round the camp bringing children into larger groups nearer the open gates. This seemed to calm some down, but others were still clearly terrified. Who were these strange new people and where were they going to take them? Thankfully for all, The Star Beings' work was made that much easier because the attention of the Watchers and Slakers was elsewhere. They were now too busy fighting for their own survival. For the

Slakers, if not the Watchers, it was a case of kill or be killed. There would be no compromising on that issue. They could never return to The Light. The Star Beings would make sure of that.

While Yula continued to heal, Arrianna did her best to pacify the children and make them less fearful. It wasn't easy. The children trusted no one. Just because they'd been turned back to The Light, didn't make things straightforward. Plenty were still fighting and struggling. They were the most difficult, but the Star Beings just held them even more gently until they were calmed.

Arrianna was finding it impossible to concentrate on the job at hand. Her mind was full of Theo. Had Kodo rescued him? Was he safe? Was everyone safe? She said a silent prayer and sent a message out for all those close to her to survive. Yula turned round and smiled at her. How could Yula remain so focused while she was being eaten up with terrible thoughts of what could be happening to Theo and those she loved? If Arrianna's stomach hadn't already been empty she would have been sick right there on the spot. She turned to see if she could catch sight of the main building, but her line of vision was blocked by other buildings. She had no idea if Kodo had been successful. Everywhere she looked the action was fierce and frantic. Insects were still shape-shifting back into Star Beings. They now outnumbered the children. She heard shouting over by the furthest part of the fencing. A gigantic struggle was taking place with the Slakers and a group of Star Beings. Nikolai was in the midst of it. Bolts of Light and Dark were zooming everywhere, crashing into bodies, smashing into the ground. Arrianna half expected help to come in the form of Kodo and the others. It didn't. The struggle went on for a long time. There were enormous white flashes as Slakers screamed their tortured last breaths. Gradually the bolts subsided along with the cessation of thousands of beating wings. The first part of their careful strategy had been a success. The children had been turned back and their tormentors had been defeated. It was the strangest sensation watching The Light start to filter and spread out over them all. Now all that had to happen was for Kodo's team to beat back Karalan and see through the second part of the plan.

Arrianna couldn't stand the tension a minute longer. She had to find out about Theo. She wasn't prepared to lose him. Not now. Yula had her back to her, healing a young boy about Theo's age. That was the deciding factor for Arrianna. She backed away from Yula and slipped quietly round the side of the wooden building. Across the heads of the Star Beings she could see the outline of the dome at the centre. She picked up her step and headed straight towards it. Her mind was as clear as it had been all day.

'Arrianna ... no!' the message came from Yula. 'Come back. Wait for the others!' Yula was already too late. Arrianna had the dome within her sights and nothing was going to stop her. She sidestepped the bodies of Watchers lying comatose on the ground and avoided any obstacles in her pathway. She bolted past Star Beings and could see the startled looks on their faces. Arrianna could even feel the necklace send out a message for her to stop. But she couldn't. Not now. No one had time to react. Arrianna was within feet of the domed building. She could hear people shouting behind her. She glanced quickly over her shoulder and saw Nikolai closing the distance between himself and her. The sweat was trickling down his forehead as he continued to run towards her. He opened his mouth and yelled in absolute desperation as loud as he could.

'No, Arrianna ... No!' She did hesitate, and Nikolai thought for a moment she was going to stop. Instead, she turned her body away and took the last few steps to the entrance of the building. She could hear haunting, blood chilling screams and violent, to-the-death clashes coming from deep within the building. There was a deep, earth-shaking rumble as brilliant flashes rose out of the dome and into the sky above. As she raised her foot onto the first stone step at the entrance, Wolf came bolting out. Arrianna stopped in her tracks when he bounded down the steps and landed on the ground a couple of feet away. He shook the dirt off his long white coat then stood still. Arrianna felt the emotion swell up inside her.

'Oh, Wolf!' she cried out. 'Thank God you're safe.' She turned to walk towards him and looked straight into his eyes. She felt the blood drain from her face. Her heart lurched and tightened in a ruthless, breath-stopping grip. She stared at Wolf in horror as fear took a stranglehold from which she could see no possible return or release.

Chapter 11

Crazy things kept running through Kodo's mind and there wasn't a damn thing he could do to stop them. When his discipline slipped and he thought of Arrianna he found it difficult to be objective. He couldn't even pinpoint when exactly over the last few days things had changed from simply being her protector to feelings which ran deeper than that. Somehow, without really trying, she'd crept under the barriers surrounding his senses. Emotions he never knew he possessed about her flooded his mind when he thought of her. It had nothing to do with Eleina; he realized that now. It was the last thing he'd wanted to happen. Because he knew the impossibility of it, it made it that much more difficult to accept. He didn't want the group splitting up and her being out of his sight in a dangerous situation. It made him feel uneasy. She'd been as brave as any of them and had done all he'd asked of her, when inside he knew she was in complete turmoil. She was terrified at the prospect of losing Theo, and all at sea over the strange new feelings she was having about himself. Reality had taken a back seat with the bizarre events which had taken over her life. She had no true understanding what was real and not real anymore. He wasn't surprised she was confused. He was confused. He knew that by sending her with Nikolai and Yula she'd at least be protected from any direct contact with Karalan and the worst of the Slakers. When he'd placed the knife in her hand, he'd wanted more than anything to share a few moments alone with her. He needed to tell her that everything would work out, but he couldn't. There was no opportunity with the others around and they'd run out of time. He wondered as he looked down onto her upturned face if it would be the last time he saw her and it tore him apart. That thought paralysed his actions into non-action. Where he could so easily have reached out and touched her he didn't. Instead he turned around and with Zorkan, Finn and Wolf he ran through the trees towards Karalan's stronghold and away from Arrianna.

By the time Kodo's group reached the outer fencing of the camp, it was already down. A group of thirty Star Beings with staffs stood beside the gaping void. Ahead of them a large swarm of hornets separated and headed straight towards the domed building. There was no need for pretence any more. Karalan knew they were coming. The protective shield he'd placed around the building was demolished in seconds as beams of powerful light shot out from the tips of their staffs. The shield crumpled and disintegrated into dusty particles and drifted down onto the ground. It was a crude attempt at a delaying tactic and it hadn't worked. Hornets swept through any entrance available to them with Star Beings in hot pursuit. Once inside, they would all make their way to the centre of the building where they were sure Karalan and his Slakers would be. They made a start. Outside the light had been bad, but they quickly discovered that inside was even worse. Away from the door it was almost pitch black. They used light from their staffs to guide them and find their bearings. Cautiously they began to spread out and infiltrate the building. Initially they were confused with the layout until they realized there was another wall directly in front of them, then another in front of that. It was like a giant maze of sections of walls at odd shaped angles. There were so many twists and turns and several routes came abruptly to dead ends. What they needed was to find a way in to the inner sanctum and not to be going round in circles like this.

Valuable time they didn't have was being wasted and frittered away. That could only be helping Karalan. He'd be putting it to good use and that would work against Kodo and the rest of the Star Beings.

The message came through from Wolf only seconds later and everyone breathed a sigh of relief.

'Found it!' They followed his thought until they found him standing to the side of an arched metal door covered with black iron studs which were shaped to look like eyes. Kodo got a bad feeling about this. He didn't like it and from the expressions on the others' faces they didn't either. Something wasn't quite right. Kodo could have sworn they'd passed that section before and there had been no door there. Now, rather conveniently, one had appeared. It was all a bit too obvious and easy.

'Stand back from the door,' Zorkan shouted, as he and Finn put their long strong legs to good use and pushed the door hard with their feet. It was as heavy as it looked and swung open slowly. There was a sudden rush of air when the hail of bamboo-shafted, steel-tipped arrows, a favourite of the Eastern Ancient Masters, shot through the open doorway where the group would have been standing. They were so powerful they either split the stone and lodged deep in the wall, or, ricocheted wildly off it. No one was hurt. If the arrows hadn't mown them down, then the spiked pit at the other side of the door certainly would have.

'Mm ... nice,' said Zorkan in disgust when he inspected an arrow tip and walked away from the door. 'I wonder what other little delights they have in store for us?' They retraced their steps and started again. The group were impatient but there was nothing they could do until they found their way into the centre. It was the hornets who finally came up trumps. If it hadn't been for them persevering to get access and squeezing through tiny gaps in the walls' masonry, they would have missed it. As they watched them busy themselves, the outline of the stone door became apparent.

'Pretty clever,' Kodo mused to himself. 'Not clever enough, though.' He and a few others put their weight behind the door and watched as it scraped across the floor and opened inwards to reveal the interior space they'd been searching for. Kodo was surprised to see just how big it was and how wide. It reminded him of a giant gladiatorial arena in waiting. He was determined his group of Star Beings weren't going to be the ones led to the slaughter. Not today, and definitely not if he could help it.

The walls of the room were thick and solid and would have been difficult to penetrate by less observant forces. They'd done well to spot it. The floor had been chipped out of limestone and was worn down with the passage of time. Dozens of candles cast their flickering shadow-light from heavy metal holders nailed into the walls. It brought a haunting, ephemeral quality to the room. Between each candle, enormous carved effigies of all that was Dark hung as reminders to those who would doubt. In the centre of the room was a raised circular dais with ancient ritualistic symbols which radiated nothing but pure evil. Everyone could feel the energy pull at them and try to suck them in. Apart from the twenty or so Slakers positioned around eight large stone columns supporting the dome in the centre, the rest of the room appeared to by empty. Where the hell was Karalan?

That thought was as far as Kodo got before the first dark bolt flashed past his head. After that it was open warfare as Star Beings pitted themselves against the Slakers. Hornets attacked, and were in turn attacked as Slakers shape-shifted and turned into birds to eat the insects. Insects shape-shifted again into large birds of prey, and so it went on until they reached the stage of large dogs pouncing on wild alley cats. Wolf attacked a black wolf and came out bloodied but on top. Everything was happening at such speed it was difficult to keep track. Most of the time it was impossible to tell who was who. The Light knew. Kodo and his group of Gatekeepers and Star Warriors needed all their wits about them as daggers thrust, arrows flew, blows fell and staffs parried. Kodo saw Finn collapse with a vicious blow from behind, but he was back up on his feet in seconds. The ultimate feud of Light over Dark was carried out in a theatre of unrivalled hatred and bitter recriminations, as Slakers saw the Star Beings they still could have been, if only corruption hadn't taken a hold. Even though the choice had been made aeons ago it was still a bitter pill to swallow. Their fighting intensified as a result. The opposing forces' skills became a testimony to their endurance and their ability to discipline mind over thought. This was controlled savagery and a battle of mind games unlike any other. The air was choked with the sound of battle and no one group had yet gained the upper hand. It felt like they'd been fighting for a long time, and they had. Several Slakers were slain and a small gap appeared in the ring's defences. Through the opening, directly in his line of vision, Kodo saw Karalan and his own Slakers with their backs to the dais. Lying on the ground at their feet was Theo. He wasn't moving. Kodo's eyes clashed with Karalan, and at that moment he declared his intent. Every Slaker was battling to protect Karalan. They weren't giving their master up easily and they were prepared to sacrifice everything if it meant his survival. Kodo knew in his heart it wasn't going to happen. What would Karalan be able to do? He couldn't shape-shift himself out of the building to some other place or some other universe. He was going to have to stand and fight to the end.

Karalan's Slakers stepped forward to fill the gaps and close the circle once more. Kodo was desperate to get to Theo but it was impossible. For every step he took forward he took one step back. Through all the bedlam he heard Arrianna's prayer. His concentration lapsed for a second. That was all the time the Slaker needed. He stunned Kodo with a blow to the head and sent him crashing to the ground. The breath was knocked out of him and he had a deep gash above his eye. The Slaker bent down low and grabbed the loose clothing around Kodo's neck. Kodo was a bigger trophy than most and there weren't many in Skerrilorn who hadn't heard of him. This appealed to the Slaker's vanity. He had a point to prove. He had to say something before he dealt the final blow. That was his mistake. His own neck was exposed as he leant down. Out of nowhere Snake appeared and slid across the floor towards the Slaker. He launched himself at the Slaker's neck and sunk his fangs deep into his flesh. The scream ran round the room as the Slaker dropped his weapon and frantically tried to dislodge Snake. It gave Kodo the time he needed to get to his feet and strike the man with his staff. Another Slaker was down and suddenly the tide was beginning to turn for the Star Beings. Snake slithered away and set about destroying further Slakers' hopes for glory.

When they were down to the last eight Slakers, Kodo knew it wouldn't be long. The Star Beings rapidly pressed home their undisputed advantage and concentrated all their remaining efforts on the Slakers now confined to the diminishing area of ground between the columns. Kodo's focus of attention was rudely interrupted when his thought waves unexpectedly picked up Yula's desperate plea as she cried out for Arrianna to stop. It shocked him and halted his advancing steps. What in the name of blazes had happened? How had she got away from Nikolai and Yula and where in God's name had she gone? Why hadn't she just stayed put? Deep down he knew of course exactly where she'd gone. Her insatiable need to know would have overridden any fears she had for her own safety. She'd be heading straight for the building, coming for Theo. What was this great need she had to always be pushing the boundaries just a little bit further? As a child he'd always loved that about her, but here, today, it was irresponsible and dangerous. It could end very badly for her. He had to stop her, or at least delay her. Kodo was the one in turmoil now as he watched the elite group of Star Warriors raise their staffs towards the hopelessly outnumbered Slakers. His eyes glanced over the Slakers one last time. He watched as they stepped backwards. They had almost reached the dais before he realized their numbers didn't add up. They were one down. Karalan was missing. The panic he felt immediately refocused his mind and set his heart pounding. Karalan couldn't have got far. The shout went up to search for him. As Wolf slunk in behind the dais and dragged Theo's body away across the floor, the Star Beings used their might and struck the pillars and the Slakers at the same time. Blistering bolts of Light shot upwards and shattered the structure of the large dome. The centre of the main dais where the Slakers had once stood started to crumble and cave in. Tremors ran deep and forced the ground to move and shift beneath everyone's feet. When the pillars cracked and fractured, dust began to slowly fill the centre of the room. Kodo was torn. He wanted to go straight to Theo, but he needed to find Arrianna. More importantly than that he had to find Karalan and destroy him once and for all. He felt the chill run down the entire length of his spine and he knew evil was still close. It could only be Karalan. There was no one else left. Star Beings were searching and guarding the large stone door, preventing anyone or anything from getting past. Kodo frantically scanned the room looking for the slightest sign which would give them a clue to Karalan's whereabouts. The movement was so small and so well camouflaged against the backdrop of the stone, he thought at first he might have imagined it. He intuitively knew he hadn't. He saw the scales of a thin black snake pull itself up and disappear behind a candle sconce on the wall. Kodo ran across the open space separating him but the snake had gone, and more alarmingly, he could see light on the other side. Karalan the snake had landed on the other side between walls and was only a short distance away from the steps of the main entrance. Kodo yelled out to anyone who could hear him.

'Karalan ... He's heading for the main door! Stop him! Don't let him get away!' At least a dozen pair of feet charged swiftly through the building after Kodo to try and stop Karalan from escaping. Immediately behind the main group several more Star Beings picked their way over the rubble. They lifted Theo's limp, young body and carried him away from the place which had seen so much death and destruction.

Wolf began to shape-shift right before Arrianna's eyes. As soon as she saw the loose, ill-fitting clothing she knew it was a Slaker. When she looked at his face her whole body responded with shock and revulsion. He was the most hideously evil thing she'd ever seen and he was shrouded in an aura of all that was Dark. It dripped off him. Even the ground he stood upon was affected as the imprints of his feet dried up and shrivelled underneath him. Ancient he might have been, but his reactions were still quick. Only a few inches taller than Arrianna, his power and physicality warned anyone to keep a respectful distance. No one with self-preservation in mind would want to go near him anyway. His head almost looked too big for his body. It was odd and dome shaped at the back and entirely free of hair. Like the Slaker Arrianna had seen with Eimar, his skin was stretched and pale. Along his eyebrow line an uneven grouping of ugly warts merged conspicuously into a deep, ulcerous ridge. The small scars on the side of his face testified to battles fought. Someone at sometime had come too close and caused damage to his nose. The tip was missing and the bone distorted. The worst feature of all was his eyes. They were opaque and vile, the irises enlarged and the blackest of blacks. Arrianna felt the full force of their chilling, invasive power. They scrutinized and scanned her face looking for any weakness to try and draw her in. She could feel her energy waver as the Slakers power held her. She was unable to move. When he lunged towards her she didn't put up a struggle. He twisted her body around and held her firmly with both arms. Arrianna's mind vaguely registered the long black staff he was holding in his right hand. She sensed rather than saw Nikolai and a few Star Beings standing some way off, unable to do a single thing. When she felt the energy of the staff, the Slaker drew it in against the length of her body. She made a half-hearted attempt to block its treacherous influence, but it ran through her anyway. In all her life she had never hated anyone as much as she did the Slaker for doing that. Her attempts at trying to pull away didn't succeed. The Slaker responded by digging his nails viciously into her upper body. The stench of his body was overpowering. When he bent his head down Arrianna wanted to retch. His breath was disgusting and sour.

'Sorry to be such a disappointment, Arrianna. You wanted Wolf and got me instead. Life's not fair, is it?' Arrianna felt his chin shake as he sniggered. 'Wolf's dead … and he's not the only one.' His voice was purposely soft and when he pronounced his 's's he made them sound like a hiss. Arrianna's body buckled when she heard the words and she knew there was more to come. 'That precious brother of yours … well, I hate to be the bearer of sad tidings, but he's gone too I'm afraid.' Arrianna knew then, in that one revealing moment, that this was no ordinary Slaker. This was Karalan. She didn't believe him. Her heart didn't believe him. She should have felt devoid of emotion at his words but she didn't. She felt nothing but unadulterated anger and a desire to punish him for his cruelty. It went against everything her parents and her Grandfather had taught her, but she could not help herself. Her mind cleared in an instant. It was no longer in neutral. Karalan pressed his slimy mouth up against her ear and she struggled to break free. She was no match for him. 'Of course, his death whilst devastating to you, makes little difference to me … Still … it's such a waste of a young corruptible life, wouldn't you agree?' He hadn't finished his taunting. 'You know,' and he drew it out, 'I've waited a long time to take something belonging to Gaelun, something precious, something he loves. I knew he'd send his beloved Star Beings to find Theo, but I didn't know you would come. Just think, if you'd only kept quiet I'd never have known.' Arrianna didn't have time to react to his provocation. He pulled her roughly and started to drag her away. She screamed and kicked and bit and even threw her head back to catch him in the face, but his grip only intensified and the staff pressed harder. Grandfather's necklace burned against her skin as she felt it respond to Karalan's staff.

'Help me!' she cried with an anguish borne out of despair and a genuine fear not to succumb to Karalan's will. She heard the commotion from the doorway as Kodo and a large group of Star Beings leapt down the steps and turned to the left to face Karalan and herself. She couldn't begin to describe the emotions she felt at that moment. Kodo was all right but what Karalan had said about Theo must be true. There was no sign of him. She continued to look at the doorway but no one else came. Her feeling of powerlessness was infinite. All eyes trained in on Karalan, and Arrianna could feel the tension in his body. It didn't stop him. He continued to walk backwards as the Star Beings spread out in front of them. She counted thirteen Star Beings including Kodo and knew it would be unlucky for someone. Who? was the question. Arrianna knew Karalan wasn't going to let her go. She glanced at Kodo for some sign but his eyes were firmly fixed on Karalan. No one said anything. Karalan was the first to make his intentions known. He brought his staff up hard under Arrianna's chin.

'If I go, she goes,' he said defiantly standing his ground. 'What would Gaelun think of that?' and he laughed. If Arrianna had had the strength she would have attacked him herself. Instead she had to put up with being manhandled by a power-seeking maniacal snake in the grass. Still no one could do anything except watch Karalan back further away. As he concentrated on dragging Arrianna she came to a decision. She'd made up her mind. She'd heard enough and been through enough and she wanted this torture over. Remembering what had got her into all this trouble in the first place, she shielded her mind and blocked out the thought. Her fingers spread out and inched forward under her jacket towards the hilt of Kodo's knife. As soon as she touched it, Kodo's eyes left Karalan. She ignored him and stared blankly ahead, trying to appear compliant and subdued. She had some intentions of her own and she had to conceal them. When her fingers finally closed around the hilt of the knife she let her body go limp and pretended to faint. She fell forward. Her body jarred as the end of the staff bruised her throat and tore at the skin. Karalan adjusted his body to take Arrianna's dead weight. She used the moment well. Knowing her own life depended on it, she pulled the knife from her waistband, then with two downwards and upwards movements, slashed the back of Karalan's fingers gripping the staff. As he struggled to regain his hold on it, Arrianna broke his weakened grasp around her upper body and dropped down to the ground and away from his feet.

Karalan was hit from all sides by forces of The Light. He tried to shape-shift and shot into the air, using every trick he knew, but his time was up. The crystals in the staffs sucked every tiny particle of Dark from his malignant, deformed soul. In one final explosive flash he was gone. The force of the flash was so great it lifted Arrianna up and sent her spinning through the air. She landed with a tremendous crash a few feet short of Nikolai's feet. For the first time in her life she saw stars which weren't galactic.

Chapter 12

The last clear memory Arrianna had was of somersaulting through the air before finally coming to a halt when she came up against an immovable force. She had no idea how long she had lain with her face pressed into the hard, unyielding soil, but realistically it couldn't have been more than a few seconds. Her perception of where she was and what was taking place around her was blunted and discordant with what was going on inside her head. The thought process she could normally rely upon to be sharp and accurate was fragmented and out of sync. The first things she became conscious of were the voices, low and initially indistinct, yet gaining in clarity and strength the closer they got to her. She heard someone moaning softly but didn't know who it was or if it was simply herself. Inside her head her fuddled brain was sending signals to open her eyes and yet somehow the message wasn't getting through. They remained stubbornly closed. She heard several people shouting and the dull vibrational echo of feet pounding towards her. The familiar sound of Nikolai was the only one she recognized. Hands were placed tentatively under her head and extra hands helped to roll her body over onto her back.

'Arrianna? … Arrianna, it's Nikolai. Can you hear me?' With great gentleness a hand moved slowly over her forehead and eased the matted strands of hair away from her eyes and mouth. The hot searing pain tore through her head and for a while she knew nothing but darkness.

The next person she remembered hearing after that was Kodo. She could sense him at the top of her head, kneeling over her. Not all her sensory abilities had been affected and she could smell the scent of him and it comforted her. A spasm in the muscle of her forearm reactivated the pain and the throbbing in her wrist became determinedly relentless. Her hand lay awkwardly by her left side with the blade of Kodo's knife half in, half out of the ground. She was gripping it for dear life. He prised her fingers open and removed it carefully, then flung it away from him across the open ground.

'It's all right. I've got her ... Just give her some space.' Kodo pulled her backwards and slipped his long arms underneath hers and around her midriff, making sure her head and shoulders were off the ground. He tried hard controlling his breathing and heart rate and bringing them back down to speed. When he'd seen Arrianna with the knife in her hand about to attack Karalan he could barely believe her courage and stupidity. Surely she didn't imagine she'd get away with it? He'd wanted to shout out 'Don't do it! For god's sake, stop!' but she wouldn't have changed her course of action. He knew her too well. Her ploy had been almost naïvely simplistic, but deadly dangerous, falling on the staff like that. When she'd fallen to the ground and rolled away from Karalan, Kodo knew she was in with a chance of survival. Now she was safely in front of him he wasn't letting her out of his sight. Not again. He slowly eased her body into his own until she was fully supported. Her long tangled mane of hair fell back against his chest and her back slumped into his upper body. Arrianna was still partially out of it, but on some level she was aware enough to sense the physical contact. Whether by accident or not, Kodo's mouth brushed against the side of her face without fully touching. He spoke so softly to her. Only she could hear the emotion and the way the words rolled off his tongue like a soothing caress. With every intake of breath Arrianna felt his chest rise and fall.

She could hear the beat of his heart and sensed the energy radiating from it. Kodo relaxed his grip on her slightly and placed the palm of his hand directly over her heart. His strength and Light surged through every fibre in her body and brought a feeling of semi normality back. Her body didn't ache quite as much. The fog in her head began to clear and at last she was able to open her eyes and focus. Nikolai and a small group of Star Beings were standing nearby looking at her. They were clearly concerned and so was she, though possibly for different reasons. There was no sign of Yula or Wolf and that really alarmed Arrianna. Something warm trickled down the side of her face. Her hand, already bloodied, reached up to find her own blood.

'You'll be fine,' Kodo said sympathetically as he turned her head sideways and inspected the wound. When he moved his fingers to wipe away the fine grit and grains of soil from around the wound's edges, Arrianna winced and pulled her head back.

'That hurt!' she accused him irritably. She knew she was being ungrateful when she glared at him. There was no return eye contact. Kodo placed a hand under her chin, turned her head back and continued to clean the wound. His voice was placatory and coaxing. He spoke to her as he would to a child.

'Shh … don't be so grumpy. Be still. Let me do this now or it's going to get infected and nasty.' Arrianna sat quietly and let him do what he had to. When he'd finished he leant back and inspected his handiwork.

'Mm … that's not bad. You'll survive. It's a pretty deep graze but it looks a lot worse than it really is.' Kodo's mouth turned up at the corners and he smiled straight at her. She noticed for the first time that he hadn't come out of this unscathed. He had some injuries of his own.

'You're going to be like a bear with a sore head for a couple of days, but that's all. No permanent damage.' It was typical of Kodo, Arrianna thought, to want to play things down. He was still looking out for her and wanting to protect her. She should have responded but lacked the energy to do so. Whether it was the fact she was now fully compos mentis or the realization she was, physically anyway, relatively unharmed, she didn't know. Shock began to set in. She had no control over it. Panic cut through her like a rapier shredding silk. In her mind she relived the final horrific scene with Karalan and what he'd said about Theo. She experienced the real physical sensation of things closing in and crumbling around her. As the muscles around the wall of her chest tightened and her breathing changed, she tried breaking away from Kodo but he wouldn't let go of her. This only made her more determined. She'd had enough of being restrained for one day. Somehow Arrianna needed to get away from Kodo, away from the noise of children crying in the camp. All she really needed was to be alone, so she tried again. Her body twisted and her hands came down onto Kodo's.

'Let go Kodo. Just leave me alone will you. Stop using strong-arm tactics like this, I hate it.' Arrianna was desperate to break free from Kodo and anything which reminded her of Theo's death. Kodo for his part refused to respond. 'For once in your life will you listen to me? I don't need you looking out for me any more. I've got to get away from this place. Don't you understand that?' Her voice was raised and she could feel the anger erupt inside her. 'I'm asking you one last time, let me go!' Her voice broke off but her struggling didn't. Kodo heard the words and saw the fear in her face. Now she was fully aware again it was time to tell her about Theo. He wanted to be sure she understood, so he still held on to her shoulders.

'Theo's okay, Arrianna. He's not dead. He's really confused and exhausted but he's not hurt. He's going to be okay. Wolf got him away from the Slakers.' The relief Kodo felt when Theo had been rescued was profound. Events could so easily have turned out badly. It took a second for Kodo's words to sink in. Arrianna swivelled her entire body round until she could look right into his eyes.

'What?' she asked quietly as she stared truth in the face. 'He's really alive?' Kodo studied her face as a whole host of emotions flickered across her eyes. He nodded then released his hold on her. Arrianna felt the breath catch in the back of her throat. She pushed herself up and momentum carried her forward until she stumbled to her feet. Her mind started racing. Where was he? Why hadn't she been able to see him? Arrianna stood still catching her breath, letting the full impact of Kodo's words sink in. She indulged her sense of relief, but at best it was short lived. Everything was suddenly compounded by the guilt she felt over those she knew must have been injured or something far worse in the quest to find Theo and free all the forgotten ones. She'd been so self-obsessed with thoughts of him she'd given little thought to anyone else. She hadn't even asked Kodo about Yula. If anything had happened to her she didn't think she'd ever be able to forgive herself. Arrianna's conversation with herself carried on in her head despite the clamour and chaos going on around her. Everyone seemed to be talking at the same time and she caught small snippets of children and Star Beings' voices drifting over towards her. Her thoughts invariably turned to Kodo and Wolf. The tragic news about Wolf was shocking and tore away at her insides. They would all regret the loss of something so magnificent and so special. And Kodo. What of him? She owed him an enormous debt which went way beyond anything she could ever hope to repay. It was a profound lesson for Arrianna in the codes of the Star Beings. It was their way of protecting those of their own seed.

Nikolai said something to her, then, when she didn't respond he stepped to one side. Arrianna saw his mouth move but she hadn't heard what he'd said. She looked at him enquiringly. A gap developed between him and the Star Beings, and suddenly, a definite shift in energy took place. There was an air of expectancy. Heads turned slowly. Eyes seeking, great tongue lolling, pads barely making contact with the ground, Wolf careered through the gap as though he was on a collision course. Arrianna stared in disbelief. There was no mistake this time. It was Wolf all right. He made straight for her and began to make distinctive wolf greeting sounds and run in circles around her legs. She fell to her knees and grabbed hold of him around the neck and let his coat brush across her face. He squirmed when she held on to him too tightly. He wasn't fond of restraint either. After a great deal of ear tugging and head stroking, Arrianna thanked him, not just mentally but verbally too for finding Theo. If animals could be embarrassed then Wolf was a candidate. He dropped his head and began to lick the blood off her sticky fingers. A murmur went up just before Arrianna caught sight of two other familiar faces, only they weren't so joyous. It was Finn and Zorkan. They looked shattered and sombre faced and they were carrying Theo. Her hand flew to her mouth as she called out his name. Everything was forgotten in her bid to get to him. She sprinted forward and ran alongside the two mighty warriors and looked down on that beloved face. When she saw him, her heart was in her mouth. He was recognizable, but only just. The clothing covering his body was in a disgustingly filthy state and his trainers and jeans were split at the seams. The backs of his hands were bruised and had ugly red weals across the knuckles. His long black hair, which he'd nurtured and refused to have cut, was caked with mud and lay flat against his head. Arrianna noticed at once his striking, spiky-lashed eyes were open but his complexion was deathly pale and he was having difficulty focusing. She waited until Finn and Zorkan laid him on the ground before she knelt down beside him. Ripping off her jacket she made a pillow for his head, then held both his hands in hers. He was so cold. Theo's eyes searched her face, wanting to believe but not sure if he could.

'Arri ... is that you? Are you really here? I'm not imagining this, am I?' His voice was hoarse and his mouth parched. His eyes didn't leave hers for a second. Arrianna didn't mind one bit. Just to hear his voice again was wonderful. The tears cut a crooked path down through the dirt and grime on her face. She leant forward and placed her wet cheek up against his.

'You're not imagining anything, Theo. I'm here. Kodo's here. You're safe. Nothing bad will happen to you now.' For once he didn't pull away from her. He needed the reassurance and something tangible to hold on to.

Arrianna spoke softly to him just as Kodo had to her. She spoke to him about familiar things, of a childhood shared, of happier times when their lives had been simple and uncomplicated. She renewed her sibling bonding with words of their future free from fear. Arrianna hadn't entirely blocked everything else out. She was still aware of the small flashes of light as groups of beautiful butterflies and fireflies shape-shifted back into Star Beings. The whole camp was alive with the sound of voices and activity. There was a new sense of purpose in the air as hope touched everyone's hearts. Star Beings went about the camp comforting and seeing to the children. No one came near Arrianna. They left her alone with Theo. She stayed holding him for a long time. Eventually she heard someone walk up behind her. A hand came down and rested gently on her shoulder. Arrianna half turned and saw Yula. She was smiling. Very quietly she lowered herself to the ground and sat opposite Arrianna. Nothing was said. She watched as Arrianna cried the horror and final threads of fear out of her body. Only then did she reach out to her. Kodo, Nikolai and Wolf had held back, but they too came forward and placed healing hands on Theo.

The mass exodus of the camp looked like it might be about to get underway. The air was throbbing with the sounds of insects buzzing and the chatter of hundreds of voices. All the forgotten ones were now gathered together in one large group. It was going to be a formidable undertaking transferring them out of the camp. The good news was that for every child there were at least two Star Beings to assist. Every child had been touched by the Light, but even so, there were many who just didn't have the strength to walk out. They were going to have to be carried most of the way to the portal. It was already turning dark and the wind had changed direction. It had become cold and it bit into the flesh. Arrianna buttoned the neck of her shirt and wrapped her arms around her middle. Kodo had met up with Finn and Zorkan and several others and a decision had been made. Whilst they went through the camp searching for any children they might have overlooked, Kodo returned to his own small group. Theo had recovered enough to be able to walk a short distance but that was all. Arrianna was worried about him. He'd not said one other word since he'd met Nikolai or Yula.

'Right,' said Kodo as he spoke to the group. 'That's us. We're definitely going. Even if it is nightfall, we're not staying in this place a moment longer than we have to. We need to get the children up and moving and away from here. This is not going to be easy for anyone of us. There's a lot of walking ahead. Still ... at least we'll be taking a straight road home this time.' Arrianna's mood lightened at the mention of home. They were finally going back. Then the full force of the words and their implication struck her. This journey home would only be the half of it. What would happen to Kodo and the others when their mission was finally accomplished? She couldn't and didn't want to think about it because she knew that whatever the outcome, there would be more pain involved. Her eyes lifted and she watched Kodo closely. Was he thinking the same thing? She knew in her heart of hearts he was preoccupied with what lay ahead of them that night. Where did he find his energy and stamina, she wondered when she saw him standing there? She felt exhausted and they hadn't even started. Even Wolf was feeling it. He lay on the ground, ears twitching but eyes closed.

Over by the main gate there were sudden shrieks of nervous laughter, followed by a chorus of loud 'Whoas.' Arrianna turned with the group to see horses, skittishly trampling the ground underfoot. There was stunned consternation. Where had they come from? Flashes of light began going off all over the camp as the industrious moths and hornets started shape-shifting into the most amazing collection of horses and small ponies. They had makeshift rope bridles, but all were without saddles. The group was speechless, but not Kodo. He was too busy laughing out loud at the antics of the Star Beings trying to calm the creatures down. It brought a smile to all their lips. He turned towards Theo and in a jocular way placed an arm along his shoulder and tried to ruffle the top of his muddy hair.

'So, Theo ... How good are your riding skills? Do you think you could handle one of those?' and he looked in the direction of the group of horses. 'Or do you want something a bit more manageable?' It was like Theo hadn't even heard Kodo. His brain seemed submerged in a deep languorous inertia. He just stared back blankly at Kodo and said nothing. His face showed no sign of any emotion. He'd always been close to Kodo, but not even he could get through the emptiness in Theo's eyes. The brief moment which should have lifted their spirits lapsed into genuine concern for Theo. Kodo glanced at Arrianna and raised his eyebrows in question. He didn't know what to say to her that would make any difference to her, so he spoke to Nikolai instead. His voice was flat, the humour forgotten. He was very matter of fact. 'Nikolai, why don't you go and get a couple of horses? Nothing too boisterous or powerful. We'll put Theo on one of them and the girls can share the other one. Are you all right with that? If I take care of Theo will you help Yula and Arrianna?' Nikolai had been such a strength Arrianna thought as he took his instructions from Kodo. Nothing much fazed him or detracted from the mission of the moment.

'Yeah ... that's fine by me,' he said and walked towards the gate to pick out two suitable mounts.

Out of the corner of her eye, Arrianna saw Finn and Zorkan again. They were with a large group of Star Warriors carrying the dead bodies of other Star Beings. That simple sight shocked Arrianna more than anything she'd seen that day. She reached out and took Yula's hand in hers. She touched Kodo on the arm and nodded in the direction of Finn and Zorkan. This was the true price which had been paid not only for Theo but the children's future freedom. It was a distressing sight for everyone, seeing the bodies draped in the loose flowing robes of these amazingly courageous people. A hush fell over the camp as the Star Warriors bore the bodies of their fallen brothers and sisters out of the camp.

Kodo wasn't the only one ashen faced. Arrianna forgot about Theo and tried to find the words for both Yula and Kodo. They had known these Star Beings.

'Who were they, Kodo?' she asked gently. 'I don't even know their names or anything about them. They gave up everything for us. What's going to happen to them?' She waited patiently until he was ready to answer. He didn't allow her to see the pain in his eyes.

'They were all forgotten ones at some time. Their risk was always going to be the greatest in a situation like this. They've never had the gift of immortality like your grandfather or myself. They came to the stars as lost souls and they found peace there. Now we'll take them home one final time and release their spirits out into the Starfields where they belong.' Kodo turned slowly away and with a downward turn of his head went to find Nikolai.

Yula's voice was so soft Arrianna had to struggle to hear her.

'He rescued four of them, you know. One of them was just like Nikolai and his name was Stephan. They were both babies when they were rescued. Stephan had been deliberately abandoned by his parents. Nikolai's were killed for their possessions crossing a remote mountain pass in Kazakhstan and he was left to die. When they were returned to Astaurias they were only months old. They grew up together and became like true brothers. Stephan's death will be bad for Nikolai. He doesn't find it easy to open his heart to anyone. I know this because I have tried.' Arrianna didn't have the chance to even turn to Yula. Kodo and Nikolai had returned leading two calm, sturdy mares. Nikolai averted his gaze from everyone.

It took quite some time before everyone in the camp got themselves organized. The darkness had closed in but the Star Beings and fireflies accommodated the change. Staffs lit up the ground while fireflies flew overhead helping to light the way. Theo sat stiffly on his horse, oblivious to everything, while Kodo held onto the reins. Neither Yula nor Arrianna wanted to ride just yet. They walked quietly alongside Nikolai, saying nothing, but feeling his agony. By the time they reached the gates there was quite a commotion. Hundreds of children, animals and Star Beings got caught up in a bottleneck of confusion. Children sat astride ponies for the first and probably the last time in their lives. Many of the very young lay in the arms of Star Beings with their eyes closed in slumber. The majority though, just wanted to get moving. For the second time that day Hawk and Raven, this time with crystals attached to their claws, rose above the crowd and flew out of the gates. It was the signal to move. Everyone surged forward and the march home got underway. Arrianna and the group were some of the last to leave. If it hadn't been such a horrendous experience full of painful memories for everyone, Arrianna might have seen the beauty in the long ribbon of Light leaving all that was Dark behind and walking back to a future.

Chapter 13

The journey back from Karalan's holding camp was just as arduous as Kodo had said it would be. Only the resilience and unstinting determination of the Star Beings to get the children to safety saw them through. Everyone had to dig deep into their physical and mental reserves to keep not just themselves going, but more importantly than that, to keep the children's flagging spirits up. At times it seemed an impossible task. Too exhausted to take another step, children would just simply sit down by the side of the road unable to go on. Even the strongest children began to falter and grow weary. There were some gutsy youngsters who, despite their fatigue, encouraged others just to walk that little bit further. One stopped and struggled to pick up a little boy who was falling further and further behind. Two beautiful Star Beings stepped forward and hoisted them effortlessly onto their backs, piggyback fashion. Arrianna and Yula witnessed a precious moment when a pony halted and neighed softly at a solitary child massaging her spindly limbs. She looked really nervous and they saw the mistrust in her pinched little face. The pony resolutely refused to move on. The girl forgot her fear and grabbed hold of its mane. She clambered onto its back and a new partnership was formed.

The surface of the road was uneven and caused a lot of problems. There were frequent stoppages but still they plodded on. Theo was becoming a real concern. Everything about him screamed of a troubled soul. He sat motionless, clutching the reins, withdrawn into the diminishing realms of his own fractured world. When his horse suddenly lost its footing and stumbled, he made no effort at all to correct his balance. If it hadn't been for Kodo's lightning reflexes he'd almost certainly have ended up under the hooves of the horses directly behind them. Arrianna could do nothing to help her brother. Not here. Not right now. Kodo had undertaken to look after him and he did. She and Yula soon got tired of trying to keep up with Nikolai. They took it in turns to rest their legs and let their horse take the strain. Arrianna didn't know which was worse: the pains she already had or the pains beginning in her calf muscles and ending in her buttocks. Tomorrow would reveal the hazards of riding bareback. Right now though, she had to use all her powers of concentration to stay awake and stay on the mare's broad back.

The sound of fractious children and the unrelenting, rhythmic clatter of hooves and hundreds of pairs of feet continued as they trudged through the long bitter night and into the following morning. Arrianna was beginning to wonder if the walking would ever end. How much further did they have to go to get out of this hellish place? Their small group stopped when Kodo stopped. He motioned to something in a dip in the landscape some distance off the main road.

'Recognize it?' he asked in a voice weighted with weariness and pointed to the partially concealed building. Everyone in the group did. They were in the valley and the building was the derelict shed. It brought back bad memories of the first Slaker they'd encountered in Skerrilorn, but, it also reminded them of Eimar and the forgotten ones she'd managed to get back out through the portal.

Their spirits lifted and their depleted energy levels felt the sudden rush of adrenalin. They all knew they were on the homeward stretch and it felt good.

Going through the portal had taken a lot longer, not least because they were at the back of the queue. Their sense of anticipation had built just watching group after group disappear in spectacular flashes of brilliant light. The rest of the day slipped away from them as horses and insects shape-shifted back into Star Beings and followed the children through to the other side. With Kodo supporting Theo and Wolf who'd shape-shifted back into Jack, the group finally took their last steps out of Skerrilorn.

It was no better an experience going through the portal a second time round. Arrianna felt as if she'd been sucked into the eye of a cyclone. When they found themselves back on the other side of the door, Finn and Zorkan were waiting for them. Little time was wasted on greetings. Together with Kodo, the three Star Warriors used their staffs and sealed the portal for good. No one would ever be able to get through it again. When the Watchers did finally come round, they'd find their access back into the real world had been cut off. The days of the abbey's cruel trade in abducting and transporting children to the Dark were over.

Arrianna and Nikolai had to practically carry Theo into his bedroom when they arrived back home. He was a mess, and like them, exhausted. They slipped off his trainers and pulled his duvet up over him. His eyes closed and it was as simple as that.

No sooner had the front door closed than the phone rang in the kitchen. Kodo picked it up.

'Yes, Inspector. Your timing's perfect. We're just in the door. No, we're all fine. Arrianna got a message on her mobile this morning. Theo's back. I know. It's great news, isn't it? We're all really relieved. What? No. He'd gone up to Alverton Abbey with a friend and they'd camped out. Typical teenager. He didn't realize there'd be all this fuss. No, she's fine. She's calmed down now, but she was pretty angry before. No, I'm sorry. She's busy seeing to Theo right now. I think we'll all have an early night. Yes, that's fine. I'll get her to call you sometime tomorrow. Okay, then. Thanks again for all your help and thanks for calling.'

Kodo's head turned when Arrianna and Nikolai walked into the kitchen. He sat, legs stretched out, under the small breakfast table.

'That was the police.'

'Yes, I heard,' Arrianna responded in a lacklustre voice.

'Theo settled?' he asked Nikolai.

'Yes, I think that's him for the night.'

Yula placed four steaming mugs of coffee in front of them. It was the first hot drink they'd had in a long time.

'So,' Nikolai asked, 'what happens now?' and looked across at Kodo. Poor Yula was almost asleep on her feet.

'What happens is,' Kodo replied, 'we all try and get some sleep. Tomorrow's going to be another hectic day.' No one needed much encouragement. They downed their coffee and rose sluggishly to their feet. It would take a lot more than one input of caffeine to recharge their batteries.

'Night then,' Yula said over her shoulder as she preceded Nikolai out of the kitchen. Arrianna stirred herself and made to move away from the table, but Kodo's hand stopped her. His expression was soft but serious.

'I need to speak to you. Just a few minutes, that's all. I promise. Then you can get your beauty sleep.' He pulled his chair closer, took hold of her hands and just sat quietly looking at her. There was so much he wanted to say to her, but now wasn't the time. She was too tired to respond. He chose his words carefully, not wanting to distress her any more than was necessary.

'Arrianna, we need to speak about Theo and what's going on with him. We're going to have to do something pretty drastic to help him. He can't walk around in the state he's in right now. You need to think hard what you want for him, what you want for yourself. Remember what your grandfather said. He can help. We can make Theo forget. If there's no improvement over the next twenty-four hours, then you'll have to do something to help him. You don't have to make your mind up right now. Sleep on it. We'll respect whatever decision you make.' To Arrianna's ears he made it sound so simple, only it wasn't. How could he remain so cool and so pragmatic over something as life changing as this? Arrianna raised her head and looked deep into Kodo's eyes. She'd been wrong about him being cool. His eyes were a mass of confusion, just like her own. She was past the stage of tears but her voice echoed the ache around her heart.

'Are you going to help me forget too?' she asked him, not really expecting him to answer. He did, and he was the gentlest he'd ever been with her.

'What is it you want to forget, Arrianna?' Her shoulders slumped. She eased her hands out of his and stood up to go.

'I want to forget the pain I'm going to feel when you're no longer here, Kodo.' Arrianna's pain was Kodo's pain and it tore through his senses. He wanted to go after her but he knew he couldn't. He couldn't stop her pain any more than she could.

The morning came early for Arrianna. All night long she wrestled with the idea of erasing everything about Skerrilorn from Theo's mind. Should she agree to it, shouldn't she agree to it? If she went ahead with it, she'd be deceiving Theo, and she didn't know if she could live with that kind of deception. Would she be able to convince him that he'd phoned her and returned home of his own volition? She sought help by trying to connect with her Grandfather in her mind, but nothing came of it. She was on her own as far as a decision went. Arrianna didn't feel in the least bit rested. Predictably, her body ached all over, her head was throbbing and she felt like hell. When she joined the others it was no better. Yula hadn't surfaced and Nikolai was back to the way he was when she'd first met him. He wasn't saying anything to anyone. Kodo had been the first up and he had seen to Theo and taken him breakfast in bed, but when Arrianna had gone in to sit with him, he'd looked straight through her with vacant eyes. She couldn't bear seeing him like that. She wanted Theo back, but not like this.

Hot showers and fresh clothing did little to raise the group's spirits. The house should have been happy but it wasn't. It was full of sadness and things left unsaid. Kodo was sitting in Grandfather's armchair with his elbows on his knees, staring at the floor. Arrianna sat on the floor opposite him. When he saw the look on her face he knew. She could barely look at him.

'Just be gentle with him. Don't let him get hurt. Promise me I'm doing the right thing?' It was a plea from the heart rather than a declaration of intent. Kodo stood up and touched her long flowing hair.

'You're doing what's best for him, Arrianna ... I promise you.' Arrianna watched as he walked across the room and down the corridor into Theo's bedroom. The door closed. She couldn't even begin to imagine what would soon be taking place behind that door.

Arrianna sat alone with her thoughts and Wolf by her side. The respite didn't last long. The phone started to ring and it didn't stop. She spent the best part of the morning phoning friends and neighbours, repeating the same story about Theo's camping excursion over and over again. She must have sounded convincing because she almost believed it herself. How easily the lie was established. Overnight she'd become a master of deception and she hated herself for it.

Kodo stayed with Theo behind closed doors for the rest of the morning. When he reappeared Theo was right behind him. The transformation was nothing short of miraculous. His eyes were clear and the colour had returned to his face. They walked out of the room together and suddenly the laughter was back in the house. Arrianna was astonished and showed it. She wanted to grab Theo and hug him but she knew he'd hate that so she didn't. She felt Kodo's eyes on her and she smiled at him in gratitude and held his gaze for a moment. That was all the time Theo unknowingly allowed her. He sauntered jauntily past with a wicked grin on his face.

'What's for lunch, Arri? I'm starving. Gotta feed a growing boy ... isn't that right, Kodo?' He patted his rumbling stomach and headed straight for the kitchen. He stopped in his tracks when he saw Nikolai, Yula and Wolf for the first time. It was something he hadn't been expecting, but he soon overcame any awkwardness. There were smiles all round, though Arrianna sensed Theo's hesitancy. Something clearly wasn't quite right. This would be crunch time for all of them. She glanced nervously at Yula and Nikolai. Had Theo remembered something? She decided to find out and made the introductions almost sound casual.

'Yula and Nikolai are travelling with Kodo ... and this little chap,' she bent down low to stroke Wolf, 'just came along for the ride.' Theo looked at Arrianna and she waited. Something was definitely bothering him.

'Isn't that the top I bought you for your last birthday?' he queried and nodded in Yula's direction. He wasn't being rude, just curious. Yula's voice rippled with laughter.

'We got soaked yesterday when we came to pick you up, don't you remember? I'd run out of dry clothes and Arrianna lent me some of hers. Is that okay?' she teased him. Theo wasn't sure which way to look. Arrianna saw the blush creep up the side of his face. He replied in as nonchalant a fashion as he could.

'Yeah ... That's cool. It looks good.' His head turned again and he looked back at Arrianna. He was frowning. 'God, what's happened to your head? That looks really painful.' He stopped mid flow as he began to realize something else. 'Come to think of it,' and he looked at the other faces in the room. 'What's been going on? You've all got bruises and injuries.' Then he rubbed the back of his own hand. Kodo picked up the questions.

'Well, we've all been in the wars I'd say, including yourself,' and laughed it off that way. 'Now ... what does everyone want for lunch?' A difficult moment was averted and talk turned to everyday things. The drama of the last few days was finally laid to rest. Arrianna had Theo back and she thanked heaven for that.

That afternoon they decided to get some long-needed fresh air. They needed a break from the house and the constant demands of the phone. The police had come to check on Theo. They feigned disinterest at the amassed injuries of the occupants of the house but were satisfied with Theo's story even if it had been recently planted into his brain. Every one donned warm clothing, piled into the car and headed off on the short journey to the cove. They walked through the dunes and out into the open and looked down onto the panoramic expanse. The whole two-mile stretch was completely deserted. It was the first time Nikolai had seen the ocean and he loved it. He looked like a child on Christmas morning opening his favourite gift. His whole face lit up and he looked genuinely happy. He ran flat out, letting the full blast of the wind blow into his face and his hair. Not to be outdone, Wolf took off and swiftly overtook him. They broke up into two separate groups. Yula was way ahead. She picked up a long piece of driftwood and stopped to draw pictures in the sand. Theo stood and watched her, then decided to join in and give free reign to his own creative talents. Kodo and Arrianna walked at a slower pace, their bodies braced against the stinging wind. They skirted the edges of the shoreline, dodging the waves of the incoming tide. They watched as the force of the sea churned up the fine strands of the bulbous-rooted seaweed and tossed it carelessly onto the expectant sand. This place held so many memories for Arrianna, but she never tired of it. Kodo knew the place well. He'd walked along the sweeping curve of the cove many times with Gaelun since Eleina had drowned. Of course it held sadness, but Arrianna and Theo seemed to be finally at peace with themselves and with the events of that awful day. They'd never forget, but they'd managed to move forward with their lives.

Kodo had been driven crazy all night thinking about Arrianna. Maybe he was over reacting, maybe it was all in his mind. He'd sensed a subtle, underlying tension gradually build up between himself and Arrianna. He was glad to finally have time alone with her away from all the others. The time was fast approaching for his return to Astaurias and he had to get everything he felt out into the open with her. They had to talk, but how to make a start was the difficult thing. If anything at all were to come out of this, he had to be completely honest with her and not hold back. At the very least he owed her that. Her back was to him. He watched as she followed a retreating wave then ran back up the little shelf when the wave turned and came back in. She stopped to skim a stone across the surface of the waves but it was too choppy and the stone sank without a trace after just two skims. Kodo came up behind her, turned her round so that he could look into her face and kissed her softly on the mouth. Arrianna closed her eyes. She hadn't been expecting that and was totally unprepared for the sensation and rush of emotion the kiss evoked. He held her, breathing in her sweet scent, feeling the softness of her skin against his own. When he let go of her they were both smiling, both caught up in the relief and tenderness of the moment. He held firmly onto her hand and they picked up their steps and continued to wend their way through the strewn debris at the sand's edges. Kodo was the first to speak, which was good for him. It took his mind off the feel and taste of Arrianna's mouth. He felt like a schoolboy on his first date.

'I need ... we need to talk about what we're both feeling. Maybe you'll find this difficult but it's important we're open with each other. You need to be a hundred per cent honest with me, Arrianna. I need you to tell me what you're thinking, what, if anything, you want from me.'

Kodo told her everything his heart was feeling. He'd never opened his heart to anyone like this before and because he wanted it so badly he was filled with doubt and thoughts of rejection. He knew what he felt for Arrianna, but worried everything had happened too quickly. She was young and as far as he knew she'd never had a long-term relationship before. There had been boyfriends but nothing like this. Did she have enough love for him to commit herself? He simply didn't know and said so. Once before he'd loved someone, but she'd never known of his love. With Arrianna he wanted her to know. What he felt for her was very powerful and all-consuming. He told her of the doubts he had. Maybe he was just too old and cynical in the ways of the world to truly believe it could work out. Kodo spoke of the consequences if their love were to move forward. He was an immortal. If he chose to give that up for her, then there could be no going back.

Arrianna was no less honest than he had been. She told him of her feelings in Astaurias and on the journey to rescue Theo. He already knew that, but needed to hear it in her voice, not just her mind. The sheer power of their feelings intensified to such a degree, it frightened Arrianna. What was just as evident was Kodo felt it too. Arrianna did have reservations. She was only just getting used to having the thoughts she did about Kodo, and now this. It was all going too quickly for her. She wanted Kodo to stay with her more than she'd ever wanted anything before in her life. She stopped walking and turned her body into his. Though she wanted to kiss him she didn't. Instead, she showed a maturity way beyond her years. She held him and spoke quietly, woman to man.

'Kodo ... I want to be with you ... you know that. All this has happened so quickly. I need time and I think if you're being honest you need a little more time too.' She saw his expression and the look in his eyes and thought for one awful moment he was going to shut her out. She pulled his head down and kissed him.

'This is all so new for me. I know what I'm feeling inside ... Listen to me, please. I'm not saying no, Kodo. I'm just saying I want you to be sure this is what you want, that you can live a life away from the stars. Is that really possible? Could you be happy living on Earth with me? Could you honestly leave Astaurias? I can't come to you. You have to come to me.' As they turned back and headed for the car, Kodo knew Arrianna had been right.

'When are you leaving?' she asked him without looking at him.

'Tonight,' he said. 'We'll leave tonight.' He sounded so dejected. She tried to remain positive, but the moment had passed.

'Then, before you go,' Arrianna stopped briefly and took the necklace from around her neck. She looked at the symbols representing each individual on the Star Council carved into the back of each star. 'Will you give this back to Grandfather and thank him. Tell him I love him.' She placed the necklace in Kodo's hand and held on to him for a moment longer. She didn't cry. Not then.

It was Christmas Eve and almost three months since the final farewells at the house. Parting from everyone after what they'd all been through was difficult. Parting from Kodo just about destroyed Arrianna. She'd changed her mind at least a dozen times when they returned from their walk, but in the end it didn't matter. Kodo left.

She cried for weeks. Even Theo was wondering what he could do to pull his sister out of the malaise she'd fallen into. Getting back into a regular routine with Theo and at University had helped, but her usual sparkle had gone.

'What's wrong, Arri?' Theo had asked that morning at breakfast. 'Tell me, please. Maybe I can help.' Of course Arrianna knew the impossibility of that. To talk of Kodo would mean divulging things Theo had no memory of.

She placed the last small gift for Theo under the tree and took herself off to bed. She couldn't sleep. Thoughts of merriment and goodwill towards all men were anathema to her. She tried. She honestly did, but inside she felt a little part of her had died. There had been no word at all from Kodo when she thought there would have been. Why did it have to be this way? She knew that any relationship with Kodo might seem improbable to many people, but she didn't care. She knew she loved him and she needed to hear that from him. No doubts. Just plain facts. She picked up Big Ted and Little Ted from the pillow beside her and felt their furry familiarity, but even they could bring her little solace. It was pointless tossing and turning, so she slipped on a dressing gown and went to make herself some hot chocolate. She sat at the breakfast table and looked out into the evening sky. There were some clouds and she could still make out a few constellations. The longing overtook her as she allowed herself to think of Astaurias and everyone there. She wanted to be near them again to feel their love and live their gentle way. Above all she wanted Kodo.

The drink warmed her stomach but she still felt chilled and headed back off to bed. Her nightlight was on and she saw that poor Old Teds must have fallen off the bed. She picked them up and went to place them back on her pillow. Her hand stopped and heart along with it. Lying in the middle of the pillow were two very different and utterly amazing things.

She lifted the single crystal star on the exquisitely spun chain and turned it over. It was from Grandfather.

'Happy Christmas, my darling girl. Wear it well, and think of me often.' The message rang loud and clear in Arrianna's mind and she felt the salt of the tears prickle her eyes. She placed the necklace around her neck and felt its warmth against her throat. Her heart began to feel it too. She leaned forward and carefully picked up the second gift. It was from Lady Samia: a perfect white feather belonging to Hawk. Arrianna held it between her fingers and brushed the feather gently across her cheek.

'Thank you,' she said silently, 'thank you.' She sat on the edge of her bed and felt the love start to grow in her heart again. She blew gently into the feather and watched as the golden tips parted then fell back into perfect symmetry.

'Just a little while longer, sweet Arrianna.' She heard Lady Samia's gentle voice. 'Be patient and hold on to your dream.' There was a pause before Lady Samia continued. Her voice was filled with laughter now. 'I have a message for you from Kodo.' Arrianna waited and waited. 'I've to tell you the doubts are gone. He's coming back home to you, maybe sooner than you think.' Arrianna's heart felt as though it would burst. She couldn't think straight. What had Kodo said? When would he be coming? Arrianna realized it didn't matter how long she had to wait. Her Star Warrior was coming home.

The End